THE SPIDER:
SATAN'S WORKSHOP

SATAN'S WORKSHOP

By Grant Stockbridge

STEEGER BOOKS • 2020

CHAPTER 1
THE RED WOMAN'S GANG

COLD PREMONITION tugged at Richard Wentworth's heart. His blood raced. Suddenly he knew that the feeling of restlessness and uneasiness he had been experiencing all that day was about to find its culmination here on Fifth Avenue at two o'clock in the morning.

Apollo, the big-boned, statuesque Great Dane with whom he was taking his nocturnal walk, also appeared to be uneasy. The great white dog, pet of Nita van Sloan, was sniffing the air, as if scenting something mysterious, unexplainable.

Wentworth's eyes narrowed as they surveyed the empty canyon of Fifth Avenue, glowing palely under the incandescence of the full moon.

There was nothing anywhere to justify that presentiment of danger which had abruptly thrust itself upon his consciousness. There was no traffic on the Avenue at this hour of the night. Patrolman O'Rourke, who should be phoning in to the precinct house at two sharp, from the corner box, was not there. But that in itself was no cause for alarm; O'Rourke might have called in a few minutes early, and then gone into some warm doorway to seek shelter from the biting cold.

Down the Avenue, across the next corner, a car was parked at the curb, in front of the Citizens' Bank & Trust Company. From somewhere nearby came the rattling and clanking of an early

1

As the Great Dane leaped after
the squat man, Wentworth's
slugs raked the car window.

milk wagon starting on its rounds. A solitary figure appeared from around the corner, pacing slowly in front of the Citizens' Bank & Trust Company, going down Fifth away from Wentworth and Apollo.

The dog growled.

Wentworth's eyes narrowed. That figure, shabbily clad in a cheap overcoat and a battered hat, was somehow familiar to him. He felt that if he were closer, he might recognize the man.

No one thing about the entire scene was sufficient in itself to arouse suspicion, were it not for his own insistent premonition, and the dog's alert restiveness. The parked car might be that of some moon-struck couple who had stopped to tell each other how much in love they were; the solitary figure might be that of a man who had imbibed too much that evening—in fact, he did seem to wabble a bit as Wentworth watched; and O'Rourke might have been at the call box and gone already.

But suddenly, all that was changed. The night began to assume a more definitely sinister aspect.

For Apollo broke the evenness of his stride, and a low growl sounded deep in his throat. They were abreast of a narrow alley between two buildings, less than a hundred feet from the corner, and the Great Dane moved away from Wentworth, his nose close to the ground, heading for the entrance to the alley.

Wentworth said, very low: "Got something, Apollo?"

The dog swung back, rubbed its cold muzzle against the back of his hand, then turned and trotted into the blackness of the alley.

Wentworth followed unhesitatingly, unbuttoning his Chesterfield almost by instinct so as to give him free access to the twin automatics he had strapped on under his dinner coat that evening.

Apollo trotted ahead, his long, graceful shape becoming only a blur in the darkness of the alley. Wentworth saw the dog halt, whimper, and lower his head. He moved up swiftly, one hand hovering at his left shoulder holster, the other flicking on the small fountain pen flashlight which he had produced.

The ray of light played about the figure of a prone man. Apollo's paw was prying gently at the man's head, as if the intelligent dog knew that its master would want to see the face. Wentworth stooped swiftly, lifted the unconscious figure. He knew, before he saw the features, who it was. The blue uniform coat of the New York Police Force told its story. He was not surprised when his flashlight illumined the bloodless countenance of Second Grade Patrolman O'Rourke.

There was blood on the back of O'Rourke's head, and there was blood on the pavement of the alley.

WENTWORTH CURSED under his breath as he lifted O'Rourke under the shoulder blades, then swung an arm under his legs and carried the man gently out of the alley. O'Rourke had been sapped from behind, then dragged in here. He was not dead yet, but if he did not receive attention soon he would not live long. Whoever had struck him down had apparently not cared whether he lived or died.

Out on the sidewalk again, Wentworth carefully eased O'Rourke down to the pavement, and stooped to examine the wound.

A low growl from Apollo caused him to raise his head. His eyes dilated with surprise. Three men had come running out of the doorway of the Citizens' Bank & Trust Company Building, down at the far corner. Two of them were carrying a heavy gunnysack between them, while the third followed close behind with a drawn revolver.

The two men with the sack ran diagonally across the sidewalk toward the parked car, while the shuffling, shabby figure of the man whom Wentworth had previously seen shouted to them, and pointed up the Avenue toward where Wentworth was kneeling beside O'Rourke with Apollo close to him. Clearly, the shabby man had been a lookout.

The two men did not stop, but hastened toward the sedan. The third man apparently did not hear what the lookout said. He continued to run, halted facing the lookout, and suddenly, as if it had all been planned beforehand, he raised his clubbed revolver, struck the lookout a vicious blow on the back of the head—just the kind of blow that must have felled Officer O'Rourke.

The lookout uttered a strangled cry, threw up his hands, and collapsed on the pavement, while his assailant stood over him as if gloating at some secret joke. This man was squat, and he wore a slouch hat well down over his eyes.

The whole thing had happened so quickly that scarcely a half-minute had elapsed between Apollo's warning growl, and the lookout's collapse to the pavement. But Wentworth's two automatics were already out, leveled for a shot at the two men fleeing toward the car with the gunny-sack.

Though Richard Wentworth was attired in evening clothes, Chesterfield and top-hat, giving the impression that he was a careless man-about-town on his way home after a night of carousing, he was far from being the type of man which his outward appearance indicated. For years he had lived in the dark and dangerous byways of adventurous crime-fighting. Through the years those twin blazing automatics had come to be portents of doom to criminals in high places, whom the law could not touch, but who were not impervious to leaden pellets.

Not as Richard Wentworth had he blazed this trail of terror

in the underworld, but as a far different
character. In order to preserve his free-
dom of movement in his own identity,
he had created another character—a
character whose name had become a
symbol of terror to wrongdoers. The
name of that character was—the Spider. Attired in hat and
cloak, with his features cunningly altered by the application of
plastic materials and pigments, the Spider had many times cut
the Gordian knot of red tape and routine which tied the hands
of law-enforcement officials.

But those very methods, unorthodox and in themselves
violent, had placed the Spider himself outside the pale of the
law. Though his name was blessed in many homes that had been
preserved from destruction, and though many a police official
entertained a sneaking admiration for him, there was, nevertheless, a reward upon the head of the Spider, and his fate would
be swift and sure if he were ever captured. He would receive as
little mercy as these bandits who were even now making away
with the spoils of the robbery of the Citizens' Bank & Trust
Company, after slugging a policeman and betraying their own
lookout.

Wentworth could easily have shot both those fleeing men
who were carrying the gunny-sack between them. His mastery
of those two automatics was a thing of perfection to behold;
and they had often stood between him and death. But even as
his fingers were about to tauten on the triggers, to send a leaden

RICHARD WENTWORTH

stream of slugs after the two bank robbers, a woman leaped out of the sedan at the curb.

She was tall, with a dark beauty that seemed to be emphasized by the half light of the moon. A long sable coat swung open, revealing her svelte figure, sheathed in a tight-fitting, deep-red dress that left her white full bosom bare and gleaming. She stepped swiftly toward the two fleeing men, and for a moment her body was interposed between them and Wentworth.

HE HELD his fire, drawing in his breath at the startling beauty of the woman, wondering swiftly what she was doing in the company of such gangsters. And in that moment the two men flung their gunny-sack into the car, drew revolvers and fired hastily at Wentworth.

Flame and thunder blasted into the quietness of Fifth Avenue, and slugs ripped the pavement close to the body of Patrolman O'Rourke.

Apollo bayed deeply in his throat, and poised on his haunches, awaiting word to launch himself in an attack against these men who were firing at his master.

The woman jumped into the sedan again, in the driver's seat. And Wentworth opened fire on the two whom she had shielded. The squat man who had felled the lookout stopped short in his

tracks, afraid to approach closer to the sedan for fear of stepping into the line of fire.

The two gunmen at the sedan were firing hurriedly, wildly; they had thought that Wentworth was a harmless passerby whose misfortune it was to have seen them making their getaway. They had thought to kill him quickly and then leave; but the sight of those two deadly spitting automatics of his disconcerted them. Crooks of this calibre are brave only when opposed by defenseless citizens. Now they were seized by panic, and their shots went wild.

The third man, the squat one, turned and ran, stumbling, around the corner. Wentworth could have shot him, but he had other plans. He wanted one of these men alive.

So he called quickly: "After him, Apollo!"

The Great Dane bayed joyously at being released for action, and his long body made a white streak of flying symmetry as he launched himself straight across the street after the squat man.

Wentworth was standing straight, straddling the body of O'Rourke, his scarf flying in the breeze, trading shots with the other two. His granite-hard face suddenly mirrored the exhilaration which battle and danger always brought to him. In that moment, as he stood there contemptuous of the bullets of his antagonists, while his two automatics spoke in quick staccato, anyone seeing him would have understood at once why an independently wealthy man like Richard Wentworth had chosen to risk his life as the Spider, rather than live in the quiet comfort of sedentary club life and social functions. It was that quality within him that has made adventurers of men in all ages and in all lands. It was that quality which sent the Vikings out across boundless oceans to unknown destinations, which sent Lewis and Clark across the unexplored plains of America through country inhabited by hostile savages. Today there were no more unknown destinations in the world, and Wentworth had turned to the profession of  crime-fighting to satisfy that longing for adventure that burned always within him.

One of the two gunmen had run around in front of the car, and was shooting from behind the protection of the radiator, while the other clung, half in and half out, one foot on the running-board, firing from behind the steel framework of the body. Wentworth shot coolly, carefully. He had only an arm to aim at, but his slug found its mark, and the man screamed as his arm fell uselessly at his side. He slumped over, and the woman at the wheel reached behind her, dragged him so that he fell in and not out.

In the meantime, the other man ran around on the outside, opened the far door of the sedan, and jumped inside. With a roar the sedan started, the woman bending over the wheel.

The rear window of the car slid up, apparently on special rollers, and a sub-machine gun was poked out at Wentworth. It began to bark in deadly grimness, but before the gunner could bring it to bear upon its mark, Wentworth's two automatics were raking the opening in the window directly above it. His slugs must have found their mark, for the submachine gun suddenly sagged, fell out of the window into the street, while a lifeless hand hung from the rear of the car.

Grimly, Wentworth lowered his sights, aimed at the tires. The car was now far down the street, almost out of range of the automatics, but a lucky shot caught the right rear tire. There was a loud, stinging explosion, and the car swerved dangerously, careened to the right, mounted the sidewalk, narrowly missing a lamppost. But the woman must have been a skillful driver indeed.

She fought the wheel, dragging the car back into the roadway, then slewed it violently around the corner, disappeared into the side street. Wentworth's eyes followed it bleakly. He was morally certain that he had killed the machine gunner, and he was absolutely sure that he had wounded the man on the running board. He was convinced there had been nobody else in the car, just those two, and the woman in the sable coat. She would not be able to get very far with one wounded man and one dead man and a flat tire. Once the police alarm was out, she would be quickly apprehended. He almost felt sorry for her.

Somehow, in spite of the fact that she was very evidently in league with these gunmen, he had a queer feeling that she was not of the criminal mold.

BUT HE had no time for speculation. The car had disappeared around the corner, and from somewhere, the clattering milk wagon he had heard a few moments before sounded closer, but registered only in his subconscious mind. His glance

12

swept around the corner, after the
squat man to whom Apollo had given
chase.

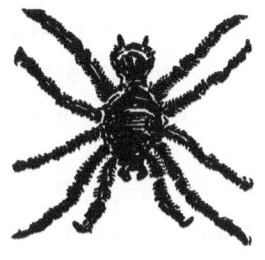

The man had halted, like a wild
animal at bay, and was leveling his
revolver at the Great Dane. The dog
had been Wentworth's companion
on many a dangerous undertaking, and he knew very well what
guns were for, and what they could do. Yet the gallant dog did
not hesitate. The squat man uttered a shriek of terror as Apollo
leaped for his throat.

The fugitive's hand tightened on the trigger of his revolver,
but the shot went wild, diverted from its mark by the man's
own panic. Apollo's bared fangs went unerringly for the other's
throat. In a second they would have clamped shut with a sicken-
ing snap, tearing flesh and jugular vein; but Wentworth shouted:
"Don't kill, Apollo!"

The dog reacted to his master's voice with the intelligence of
any human being. His great head twisted to one side in mid-leap,
and he struck the man's shoulder, sending him staggering backward with the Great Dane on top of him.

The gunman twisted out from under Apollo, raised his gun
arm, bending his wrist so that the muzzle was pointed at the
dog. And Wentworth, racing toward them, called out: "If you
shoot that dog, I'll let you have it between the eyes!"

The threat in Wentworth's icy steel voice was more definite
than the two automatics which he held. The fugitive let the
revolver drop, and got to his knees, raising both hands above his

head. Apollo backed away from him, moving so that his fore-paws guarded the dropped revolver on the ground.

The man whimpered: "I give up, mister. Don't shoot!"

Wentworth's eyes were bleak, merciless. He remembered the still form of Patrolman O'Rourke, left to die in the alley; he remembered the pitiful figure of the lookout, whom this man had struck down, to lie there until the police came. This squat man was a thug of a type to whom mercy should never be shown. He had planned to destroy some one by the lowest form of betrayal known to the Underworld—leaving him there to "take the rap" for the others.

Wentworth had in mind a grim sort of retribution for this man—a retribution that would be most just in its irony. He waited till the other was on his feet, then said: "You can put your hands down."

The man looked at him queerly, almost unbelievingly, but obeyed. His small eyes flickered with a strange, sly look as he saw Wentworth quickly return his two automatics to their holsters. He could not believe that Wentworth was deliberately leaving himself without a weapon. Swiftly his hand darted into his coat pocket, came out with a vicious-looking blackjack suspended by a leather thong. He raised his arm, stepped in past Apollo, with the intention of bringing the slungshot down on Wentworth's head.

Wentworth's lips twisted in a grim smile. "Just what I thought you'd do!" he murmured. He sidestepped with the agility of a cat, while Apollo growled deep in his throat, set himself to leap at the attacker. But the dog's assistance was unnecessary.

Wentworth's hard, bunched fist came up in a short, terrific jab that caught the squat man squarely on the chin. There was the ugly crack of knuckle on bone, and the man's head was jerked back with dreadful force. Teeth ground together, choking the grunt of pain in the other's throat. Blood spurted from his nose, and he collapsed like a deflated balloon, dropping heavily to the pavement.

THUS FAR there had not been the faintest sound of a police siren or whistle. If there was a cruising radio car in the vicinity it must certainly have heard the rattle of revolver and machine-gun shots, but it must be wandering aimlessly, seeking the direction from which they had come. In the meantime, Wentworth worked quickly.

He stooped, and seized the unconscious man by the feet, dragged him unceremoniously around the corner. He dropped him close to the body of the lookout, who lay still, with his hat smashed down upon his head where he had been struck.

Now, Wentworth turned the unconscious lookout over on his back, bent and looked into his face. Recognition glowed in his eyes.

"Laskar!" he murmured. "Ben Laskar!"

He knew the man. Laskar had been a big-time bookmaker on Broadway for a number of years, until he had become involved in a killing in a hotel room. Suspicion pointed to the unfortunate bookmaker, and Laskar had been convicted and sentenced to ten years in State's Prison. Six years had passed, and Laskar had won a pardon. Wentworth knew that the man had been released from prison, as he made it a point to know most of the goings-on in the underworld. But he had not known where the bookmaker had gone. And now he turned up, as lookout for a gang of bank robbers.

The door of the bank was open, and did not appear to have been forced in any way. Wentworth's forehead creased. How had these men gotten the door open without forcing it, and how had they avoided the ringing of the burglar alarm system? Suddenly he became sure that there was more to this than an ordinary bank robbery. A strictly professional affair would not have been carried out in this manner—and the robbers would have carried off more than one gunny-sack of loot. Also, there would have been at least a dozen gunmen, and they would have had an elaborate getaway planned.

Wentworth glanced down speculatively at the still form of Laskar. The man needed medical attention. Also, if he were found here, he would be given short shrift by the police. There was a story behind the man—a story that might lead Wentworth on a trail of adventure.

Abruptly, he caught sight of a milk wagon turning the corner into Fifth Avenue, while at the same time the scream of a police siren sounded from the east. The radio car was on its way. It was time for Wentworth to disappear from the scene. He had originally intended to leave the double-crossing squat man beside the body of the unconscious lookout, to "take the rap" with him. Now a refinement of that idea occurred to him.

"By Jove, Apollo," he exclaimed to the Great Dane who had been watching him with affectionate eyes, "By Jove, I'll do it!

You know, I think this is a big thing—bigger than any ordinary bank robbery. And we ought to sit in on it. Eh, Apollo?"

The Great Dane blinked his eyes, and stretched his paws out in front of him, bobbing his head as if in assent.

"Okay, Apollo, I'm glad you agree!"

Wentworth's idea had taken shape with the appearance of the milk wagon. Its driver had taken in the scene before the bank, with startled eyes, and he was veering over toward the corner the better to see what had happened. Wentworth waved to him and the milkman pulled up close to the curb, staring with wide eyes from the two unconscious men on the pavement before the bank to the prostrate figure of O'Rourke further up the street. He had no fear of Wentworth. Somehow, the sight of a man garbed in evening clothes and a top hat does a lot to instill courage.

The police siren was drawing nearer, and Wentworth called out urgently: "There's no car in the neighborhood, and this man is badly hurt. Will you take him to a hospital?"

Before the milkman could reply, Wentworth had lifted up the inert form of Laskar, and loaded him in through the side opening in the wagon.

The dazed driver demanded: "W-what's happened here, mister?"

Wentworth leaped up into the wagon. "It was a holdup! The robbers got away, except for that one on the ground. Hurry. This man needs first aid!"

"B-but what about those others—this fellow on the sidewalk, and the policeman over there—"

"They'll be all right. The police car is coming, and they'll have an ambulance here in no time." While he talked, Wentworth seized the reins, and clucked to the horse. "Giddap!"

The horse broke into a shambling gait, and Wentworth tugged at the left hand rein, pulled him around in a wide circle into the side street heading west, while Apollo followed along beside the wagon.

The milkman had allowed the reins to be taken from his hands, but now he protested suspiciously: "Say-ay, mister! What's the big idea? We better wait for the cops—"

"Sorry," Wentworth clipped. "That's impossible!"

The milkman lunged for the reins, and Wentworth said softly: "Sorry again, old man. This is absolutely necessary!" And he brought up his fist in a swift uppercut that caught the milkman on the chin, sent him sprawling back among the milk bottles, to stumble over the still form of Laskar and crash to the floor of the wagon.

WENTWORTH CAST a quick glance behind him to make sure that the milkman was not badly hurt, and then turned all his attention to driving the wagon. If he made an incongruous sight at two in the morning, dressed in evening clothes and tall top hat, driving a milk wagon through the streets of New York with a pure white Great Dane trotting beside it, he didn't care.

He headed west till he reached Eighth Avenue, then turned north toward the apartment house which he owned and operated, and where he had a private garage in the basement. Once he got the milk wagon in there, he would be safe.

Once he passed a policeman trying doors on his beat, and the policeman did not throw him a second glance. Wentworth took the precaution of standing well back in the wagon, so that he would be as inconspicuous as possible. And Apollo, wise dog that he was, did not follow close to the wagon now, but kept pace with it along the sidewalk.

Radio car sirens were sounding from several directions now. The alarm had at last been spread. Now the police cars all over the city would be cruising in and out of side streets and avenues, with sharp eyes out for any irregularity. That sedan with the woman driving, and with the one dead and one wounded man in it, would be spotted at once—if it had not already been deserted by its occupants. Likewise, the phenomenon of a milk wagon being driven up Eighth Avenue by a man in evening dress would not be allowed to pass without investigation.

Wentworth let the reins hang from their peg, and the horse ambled along, dropping to a walk, and moving over to the curb from force of habit. Apollo continued to pace it, sticking close to the clattering wheels. Wentworth leaned over the side, called out: "Move away, Apollo!"

The Great Dane looked up at him, and one could have sworn that the intelligent eyes of the big dog understood that he did not want to attract undue attention.

Apollo obediently dropped behind, allowing the horse and wagon to get some fifty paces ahead. No one observing them would have suspected that the dog was connected in any way with the wagon. A policeman might have wondered at the fact that such a valuable animal should be loose in the streets at this hour, but he would have found it impossible to get close enough to inspect the license plate on the collar.

Wentworth moved back into the wagon, stepping carefully over stacks of milk bottle containers, and over the inert body of Laskar. He stripped off his top hat and Chesterfield, and then his evening jacket, starched shirt front, bow tie and trousers.

Then he stooped and removed the white coat and trousers of the unconscious milkman, donning them himself. Working swiftly, he managed to get his own trousers and overcoat onto the milkman's body, and then he returned to take the reins.

He was none too soon. The wagon was swinging into Columbus Circle, and Wentworth tautened as he saw a radio car cutting across the Circle toward him. The radio car swung around and came up alongside the wagon.

Wentworth's eyes narrowed. Some one might have seen him leaving the scene of the crime; some one looking out from a window might have phoned a tip to headquarters. His right hand stole under his milkman's coat to one of the holstered automatics, into which he had inserted fresh clips.

If the police attempted to stop him, he would not fight it out with them. He never shot an officer of the law, no matter how dangerous his position might be. These men were only doing their duty. It was not their fault that the authorities had set a price upon the Spider's head. Wentworth had no quarrel with them.

But if they tried to stop him now, he could place a couple of slugs in their tires and attempt to escape. How successful that attempt would be, in the slow-moving milk wagon, was a question he could not answer. He wished at the moment that some other vehicle had presented itself in front of the Citizens' Bank & Trust Company.

The man next to the driver of the radio car leaned out of the window, and called up to him: "Say, feller!"

Wentworth glanced down at him, his hand close to his shoulder holster. "Hello, officer."

"Did you see any suspicious looking cars pass you in the last couple of minutes?"

Wentworth breathed a sight of relief, let his hand slip away from the holster. "No, officer, nothing passed me either way, except a couple of taxicabs, and their flags were up. Why? Anything doing?"

"Bank robbery!" the officer told him curtly, and the car pulled away, turned right and headed across Fifty-ninth toward Fifth Avenue.

WENTWORTH SIGHED, and continued around the Circle, and into Central Park West. He passed another milk wagon coming out of one of the side streets, and the driver waved to him. Wentworth waved back, and drove on. Glancing over his shoulder, he could see the other driver staring after him. The man no doubt was wondering where he belonged. Fortunately, the other wagon was that of a rival milk company, and its driver would not be in a position to check up too closely.

At last, Wentworth reached the street where his house was located, and swung into it. Now came the ticklish part of the business. There was a driveway alongside his house, leading to a row of garages in the rear, maintained for the convenience of the tenants. But Wentworth was the landlord, and those garages

21

were more for his own convenience. Four of them were reserved for him. Once he was in there, he would be safe from detection. But, if anyone observed the milk wagon entering one of the garages, it would arouse enough suspicion to cause an investigation by the police. He must be careful.

His eyes darted up and down both sides of the street as he drove along, going slowly so as to avoid as much noise as possible. He knew from his own experience that when one is up during the early morning hours, nothing sounds so loud as the rattle of a milk wagon in the street.

A solitary man was coming toward him from the other end of the block; otherwise the street was deserted. Wentworth swung into the alley, drove to the rear and pulled up before the row of garages across the back.

He descended from the wagon, unlocked the door of number three, and led the horse in, quickly closing the door after him.

Garages numbers one, two, three and four were different from the others in the row in only one particular—there was a trapdoor in the floor of each, leading down into a passage that connected with the basement of the house. From the basement, a private self-service elevator carried one directly up to the penthouse apartment of Richard Wentworth. Another fact with which none of the tenants was familiar was that the rear walls of garages numbers one, two, three and four could slide up to allow one egress into another alley, alongside a church facing on the next block. It was a perfect means of escape in the event that the owner of the house should at any time be cornered here.

Wentworth now stepped over to a corner of the garage,

stooped, and ran his fingers along an edge of the floor close to the wall. He found a button flush with the floor, and pressed it. At once a section of the floor about a foot square opened on hinges like a miniature trapdoor, revealing a recess in which lay a small box of emergency tools and make-up, resting beside a small size French phone like those sold for the use of boys who wish to install their own toy phone systems at home. The only difference was that this was not a toy.

Wentworth lifted the receiver, and in a moment he was connected with his apartment on the roof of the building.

"Ram Singh!" he said crisply. "Come down to Garage Number Three by the basement passage. And bring Jackson!"

The voice of Ram Singh, his Sikh servant, came to him over the wire: "Allah be praised! We had begun to worry for thee, master. There was news over the radio—"

"Never mind that now," Wentworth broke in. "I'm safe and sound. Come down quickly. And one of you go to the front door and let Apollo in."

Ram Singh and Jackson were much more than servants. They had been with Wentworth for years. The Sikh came of a fighting line of warriors in India, and his fierce pride permitted him to bow to no man—except to Richard Wentworth, whom alone he deemed worthy of being his master.

Jackson, the chauffeur, had served with Major Wentworth in the World War in France, and he still gave him the same unquestioning obedience and admiration that the sergeant had accorded the major in the old days. These two were among the select few who were privileged to know that Richard Wentworth

23

and the Spider were one and the same person; and Wentworth's secret was as safe with them as if it were locked in the vaults of the Bank of England.

There had been several occasions in the past when both Ram Singh and Jackson had been offered dazzling bribes, had been faced with unspeakable tortures, if only they would speak some word that would betray their master. Wentworth knew that they would allow their tongues to be cut out rather than talk. And if these two men gave him more than ordinary allegiance, Richard Wentworth repaid that loyalty a hundredfold by the trust he placed in them.

It was only a few minutes before Ram Singh and Jackson appeared in the garage through the trapdoor cunningly fitted into the exact center of the floor, where it would open directly underneath any automobile which might be stored here.

Ram Singh, huge and bearded, chuckled at sight of Wentworth attired as a milkman. "In your time, master," the big Sikh rumbled into his beard, "you have been many things to many men. But never have I known you to be a seller of milk. Perhaps you can also supply us with some fresh cream cheese, and maybe an egg or two?"

Jackson's wooden face also cracked into a smile as he surveyed the milk wagon. "Does the Major intend to take a milk bath this morning? Would you like the milk cold, or with the chill taken out of it, sir?"

"Never mind the wise-cracks, you two!" Wentworth grinned. "Leave the milk right here, and help me to carry those two gentlemen upstairs!"

He pointed into the interior of the wagon, and both men gasped when they saw the unconscious figures of the milkman and the man, Laskar.

"Where did you get them, sir?" Jackson asked.

"At the Citizens' Bank & Trust Company," Wentworth informed them. "The bank was robbed tonight."

"We got it on the radio, sir."

Wentworth nodded. "The man you're lifting out now was the lookout for the robbers. They double crossed him—knocked him on the head and left him to be found by the police."

Ram Singh, who had heaved the milkman to his shoulder, showed his teeth in a grin as he stepped through the trapdoor. "And you abducted him in the wagon of the milk seller!"

"That's right, Ram Singh. I know the man. It's damned funny that he should have been there at all. I think there's something big in the wind, and I want to question him privately, without the police interfering."

"Allah be praised!" the Sikh intoned as he disappeared down the ladder with his burden. "Perhaps we shall see action once more!"

CHAPTER 2
THE SPIDER'S WEB

WENTWORTH'S PREMISES on the roof of the Hopecrest Apartments consisted of eleven rooms, on two floors. The penthouse itself occupied fully half of the roof space, and the other half was landscaped, with beautifully cultivated lawn, and two aisles flanked by umbrella trees. The private elevator opened into a small foyer in the lower of the two floors. Otherwise, the only access to the place was from the public elevators, across the lawn. Close inspection would have revealed that all the windows were of bullet-proof glass, and in addition fitted with steel shutters that could be closed at a moment's notice by merely pressing a button from inside.

Each of the shutters was provided with loopholes for rifle fire, by means of which any attacking force crossing the lawn could be effectively enfiladed.

Photo-electric rays, set at various angles around the lawn and the paths leading to the apartment, gave ample notice to those within of the approach of any unannounced party.

To the uninitiated, such precautions might have appeared silly; but out of the experiences of Richard Wentworth and of Ram Singh, Jackson, and Wentworth's old butler, Jenkyns, every bit of protection with which this place was surrounded was a grim, bitter necessity.

In the past, the Spider had pitted himself against some of the wiliest, most cunning and ruthless criminals of the decade. And he knew only too well that the enemies he had made in the past were ever seeking to discover the true identity of the person whose blazing automatics had wreaked such havoc in the Underworld. There were many men who would have esteemed it a privilege to bring about the death of the Spider, and those men were by no means lacking in intellect and in resources.

For Wentworth had always chosen to fight those criminals who appeared the most dangerous and the most potent for

evil. Many of them were dead, many in
prison; but there were others who had
fled, and whose vengeful ego would
surely bring them back to even up the
score with the man who had been their
undoing.

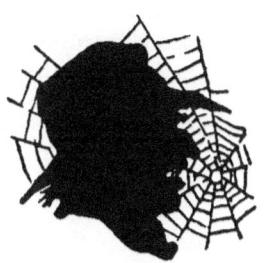

On occasions, such criminals had
shrewdly put two and two together,
and guessed that Richard Wentworth was the Spider. More than
once, the Spider's domicile had been attacked, once with almost
disastrous results. So that now, this penthouse apartment was
built, equipped and supplied to withstand a siege if necessary.

After returning from his adventure at Keystone City,* Wentworth had made use of his leisure time to buy this piece of
land near Central Park West, and to supervise personally the
construction of the Hopecrest Apartments. Being a man of
independent wealth, he had been able to build without stint-
ing. The foundation was twice as deep as the foundation of the
average house of its type; all the fittings were of the best that
money could buy; the steel and concrete work were more calcu-
lated for a fort than for a dwelling, and the outer doors of the
building were of sheet steel, so cunningly disguised that they
resembled opaque glass, embroidered with delicate scroll work.
Yet, if necessity arose, those doors could be instantly shut, and
remain shut in the face of anything short of a ten-inch gun.

The elevator operators, the porters, the doormen, were all

* AUTHOR'S NOTE: For an account of the adventure referred to above, see
"The Mill-Town Massacres."

ex-soldiers, recruited wherever possible from Wentworth's own battalion in the World War. They received pay far out of proportion to the type of work they performed; but each was furnished with a service revolver, and was prepared to use it at his employer's order. There was not a single man employed at the Hopecrest Apartments with whose life history Wentworth was not thoroughly acquainted. These men did not share Ram Singh's and Jackson's knowledge of their employer's dual personality, but they did know that Richard Wentworth was a man to whom it paid to be loyal; and from their previous knowledge of him as their officer in the front lines, they were quite sure that whatever he called upon them to do would not be dishonorable.

The tenants of the sixteen-story apartment house were also hand-picked; and with characteristic daring, Wentworth had rented a suite on the tenth floor to Stanley Kirkpatrick, Police Commissioner of New York City. District Attorney Baldwin occupied the eighth floor, and John Collingsby, Senior Judge of the Court of General Sessions, the twelfth. An ex-senator and two other judges were among the other lessees in the Hopecrest.

And even now, while these eminent jurists and guardians of the law were comfortably asleep in the building, their landlord was busy in his penthouse apartment with matters that would have turned their hair gray had they known how he was handling them—or, for that matter, that he was handling them at all.

IN A small room, equipped as an office on the upper floor of the duplex apartment, Richard Wentworth sat at a desk, opposite the unfortunate milkman whom he had virtually abducted from in front of the Citizens' Bank & Trust Company, and whose wagon he had stolen. The man was still nursing his jaw, where a livid mark still showed from the blow he had received. He was a well-built man, in his early forties, with a sparse crop of nondescript hair, and almost colorless eyes which reflected a peculiar mixture of wonder, puzzlement, and perhaps a little fear. He sat on the edge of the chair, attired in a new suit taken from Wentworth's supply closet, and from which all identifying marks and makers' tags had been removed. He was twirling a hat nervously between his fingers, and blinking into the bright desk light which had been so arranged that it shone full in his face, leaving his interrogator completely in shadow, virtually invisible. Should this man ever be called upon to identify his abductor, he would have to call upon his memory of the short few minutes in the milk wagon; and the odds were all against his being able to pick the right man.

Wentworth spoke to him now, deliberately pitching his voice in a slightly higher scale than that which he ordinarily used.

"What is your name?" he demanded.

The other shifted nervously in his seat, glanced almost apprehensively behind him, then turned to blink into the bright light once more.

"Frank Donley—sir!" He added the "sir" reluctantly, as if against his better judgment. Then suddenly, summoning up his courage: "Look here, mister, you can't do this to me! I'll have the law on you! By God, it's robbery, an' it's kidnapping, that's what it is. I'll get the G-Men after you. Where do you get your nerve—"

29

"*Stop, Donley!*" Wentworth's harsh, authoritative voice cut into his protestations.

Donley subsided, shrinking in the chair. He was a meek man, used to taking orders; and this voice sounded as if it belonged to some one who was used to *giving* orders. He gulped, became silent.

Wentworth went on. "You've already been told, Mr. Donley, that no one here means you any harm. You have been treated well, haven't you?"

Donley fidgeted. "We-ell, I've only been here a few minutes—maybe a quarter of an hour. I come to while that guy with the beard was carrying me into a room. I tried to kick, an' he just held my hands, like I was a baby. But outside of that, I got no kick coming, mister. These clothes are pretty good—"

"Of course," Wentworth interrupted, "I want to apologize to you for the way you were treated in your wagon. Believe me, it was absolutely necessary to knock you out. But you shall be reimbursed for any inconvenience to yourself, as well as for any pain which has been caused you."

"Reimbursed?" Donley blinked. "You mean—I'll be paid?"

For answer, Wentworth drew a sheaf of bills from the drawer of his desk, and slid them over toward the milkman. "Count them!" he ordered.

Donley picked them up gingerly, saw that the top bill was a ten-dollar note, and gasped. Quickly, eagerly, he ruffled through them. "Why—why, there's *five hundred dollars here!*"

"That's correct. It's all yours—to do with as you please."

"Y-you mean—I can go now, and you'll give me back my wagon, and let me take this money—"

"Not exactly. For the time being, it is necessary that you should leave New York. You will be taken to a country estate, where you will receive the best of treatment, the best of food, and the best of entertainment. You must remain there for at least a week, perhaps for two. It will be a complete vacation. At the end of that time, you may return, and you will receive another five hundred dollars. How does that strike you?"

"B-but my job—"

"You work for the Health Foods Milk Company, don't you?"

"Y-yes, sir."

"You're married?"

"Yes, sir. Two children—"

"I will guarantee that your job will remain open, that your employer will take you back, and that your family will receive a substantial sum each week that you are away—far more than you earn on your job."

"B-but why do you offer me all this?"

"Because I find that I will have use for your milk wagon. Also, because I do not wish you to be available for police questioning for a while."

"But the police will probably arrest me when I come back. That was a robbery, at the Citizens' Bank & Trust Company. For all I know, some one was killed. And me, running away like this, they'll think I had something to do with it."

"No one will connect you with the robbery, because you weren't seen near the bank."

Donley shook his head. "No, sir. You can do what you like to me. I've been an honest man all my life, and I won't start breaking the law now, not even for a thousand dollars. Why, come to think of it, you must be a crook of some kind. You must of had a hand in that robbery!"

"I assure you that I am not a crook, and that I had nothing to do with the robbery. In fact, I am turning all my energies to discovering the perpetrators of that crime."

Donley sneered. "How do I know you're speaking the truth, mister? You *say* you ain't a crook, but that don't *prove* nothing. All I know is, I saw you at the scene of the robbery, an' you stole my milk wagon an' made a getaway in it. You *say* you'll take care of my family, and get me back my job, but that's no guarantee. Who are you, anyway?"

WENTWORTH SIGHED. "I suppose I'll have to convince you." He paused a moment, while Donley waited, wondering at the strangeness of the things that had happened to him so far.

Wentworth went on, his voice becoming almost casual, as if he were changing the subject. "Have you been reading in the newspapers about the crime wave that has been sweeping the city recently?"

Donley nodded. "Sure. They say there's some new criminal that must be operating on a big scale. All those important people being kidnapped, like Anne Hale, the actress, and Morgan Johnson, the banker, and Dr. Peter Humphries. Morgan

"Let me upstairs—" He stopped, frustrated. The gate was down again.

Johnson was the only one who came back. I saw in the papers that he was found only the other day, unharmed, and he's been back at work—*say!*"— abruptly, Donley's face flushed as an idea struck him—"*Morgan Johnson is the President of the Citizens' Bank & Trust Company!*"

"That's right," Wentworth said drily. "I was wondering how long it would take you to see the connection."

"Then—then Morgan Johnson's kidnapping had something to do with the robbery today—"

"I don't know yet, Donley. That's what I want to find out. But let's get on with our talk. You've read, no doubt, about how Anne Hale, the actress, was snatched out from under the eyes of a stage door crowd at the Oriental Theatre?"

"Yes, sir. Men with machine guns held the crowd back—"

"And you've read about how Douglas Fenner, the producer of her play, appealed for help?"

"Yes, sir. He published an advertisement in the paper, begging the Spider to find her. The ad's been appearing every day for a week. He promises to donate ten thousand dollars to any charity the Spider names if he brings her back."

"Do you think the Spider will take him up?"

"I hope to God he does, sir!" Donley exclaimed fervently. "Anne Hale is a great actress. And if anybody can find her, that man is the Spider. He don't worry about writs of *habeas corpus,* and search warrants, and such like. He goes and blasts the living daylights out of the crooks. Why, look what he done in Keystone City. If it hadn't been for him—"

"Yes, yes, I understand," Wentworth broke in quickly. "Now, tell me—if the Spider were to need your help—would you give it to him?"

"With all my heart, sir!"

"In spite of the fact that the police don't approve of his methods, and in spite of the fact that it might get you in wrong with the law?"

"In spite of everything, sir. I want to tell you, no matter what the police think of him, there's millions of plain people all over the country that bless his name. He's done more good—"

"All right, Donley. I understand just how you feel, and I thank you for the sentiments."

Donley stared into the blinding light on the desk, his jaw suddenly going slack. "*You* thank me, sir?"

Wentworth said nothing. But he slowly removed from his pocket a platinum cigarette lighter, flipped open the bottom, and pressed the open end upon a pad of paper lying on the desk. There appeared on that paper a small reproduction of a spider, drawn in blood-red lines. It was a symbol known throughout the country. Wherever vicious criminals had been found dead, killed by the blazing automatics of the Spider, there had also been found upon their foreheads that small, eloquent seal, so that all might know that the Spider had exacted final retribution from them. There was not a man, woman or child in New York who was unfamiliar with the insignia.

He pushed the pad of paper across the desk, so that the light from the lamp fell upon it.

The milkman's eyes dilated.

Wentworth said slowly: *"It is the Spider who asks your help now, Donley!"*

For a long minute of time there was utter silence in the half-darkened room, while the truth dawned upon Frank Donley—the truth that had begun to simmer upon him during the last few moments of the conversation.

This man, facing him across the desk, invisible because of the glaring light, *was the Spider!*

Much of the events of the morning became suddenly clear to him.

NOW HE understood why he had been reluctant to believe this man a criminal, even though all the circumstances had pointed to that conclusion. He leaned forward in his chair, his face expressive of deep-felt emotion.

"Mister," he said in a voice that shook with sincerity, "I'll do anything you say. I—I didn't know you were the Spider!"

"Good. You will be taken to the place in the country that I spoke of, and you will stay there with the bearded man who carried you upstairs. Here's a pencil. Write down the address of your family, and send them a short note, saying that you are all right. I will see that they are taken care of, and supplied with funds. And when you return, I will see that you are given back your job—or that you get a better one."

Donley penciled the note without hesitation. And while he wrote, Wentworth pressed a button on his desk which summoned Ram Singh, then went on: "It will be necessary to blindfold you when you leave. You do not know the location of this place, and it is best that you should remain in ignorance of it—so that if you are ever questioned by the police, you will not have to tell any lies."

Donley finished writing, and Ram Singh entered.

Wentworth issued swift instructions to the Sikh in Hindustani, telling him to take the milkman to his estate in Westchester, and to keep him there.

Ram Singh groaned. "Inshallah, master! Must I then, remain in the country, being a wet-nurse to this seller of milk, while there is fighting going on here? Send one of the others—"

"No, Ram Singh, I want you to go. But you need not stay there. Leave this man in charge of Sergeant Reilly, and return."

Sergeant Reilly was a one-legged veteran whom Wentworth had placed in charge of the place in Westchester, and whom he felt would be well able to take care of Donley.

Ram Singh showed his white teeth in a happy grin. "That is better, master. I go."

He took Frank Donley in tow, and led him from the room, after tying a bandage about his eyes. When they were gone, Wentworth rang for Jackson, who appeared instantly.

"How's Ben Laskar?" he asked.

"He's all right, sir," Jackson reported. "We patched up the gash in his head. He's a little dazed, but otherwise all right. According to your instructions, we told him he was in the hands of the Spider, and to get ready to spill his story. He understands that he was double-crossed by his pals, and he's willing to talk."

"Very well, bring him in."

While Jackson was gone to fetch the unfortunate lookout, Wentworth went swiftly over the situation in his mind. More than five months ago, the mysterious kidnappings of which he had spoken to the milkman had begun. They had all been ingeniously arranged, giving evidence that no ordinary gangster was behind them. Half a dozen wealthy, important people had been abducted, and there had been no trace of them until the other day, when Morgan Johnson, the president of the Citizens' Bank & Trust Company, had been found, lying in the street in front of his home, apparently none the worse for his experience.

The city was full of G-men, and they were taking full charge of the case, but Wentworth had managed to learn that Johnson bore the scars of several operations. Why those operations had been performed, Johnson could not tell, and the Department of Justice was at a loss to assign any motive for the kidnapping, since no ransom notes had been sent to Johnson's family or bank, or to the families of any of the other kidnapped persons.

The relatives of the other kidnapped people had begun to give up hope of ever seeing their beloved ones again, but when the president of the Citizens' Bank was found, hope blossomed again. Douglas Fenner, the producer of Spanish Afternoons, the play of which Anne Hale had been the star before her abduction, published an appeal in all the newspapers, asking the Spider to help find her.

Wentworth had hesitated to approach Fenner for any information, because the police had immediately set shadows upon the producer, in the hope of trapping the Spider. He wanted badly to talk to Fenner, but he had never met the man before, and had no legitimate reason for approaching him.

HIS THOUGHTS were interrupted by the entrance of Jackson, with Ben Laskar. The little bookmaker was nervous, and obviously ill at ease, as he seated himself in the chair opposite the desk, and lowered his eyes before the blinding light. He raised a hand to touch the bandage on his head, shifted uncomfortably in the chair, and looked almost wistfully after Jackson's broad back as it disappeared through the door.

Wentworth, still invisible behind the light, waited until the door was closed, then spoke. "Laskar!"

The bookmaker turned and faced the light, summoning up his courage. "Yes?"

"You know who I am?"

"Yes. They told me. You're the Spider. I want to thank you for what you did for me. I know that those muggs sapped me and left me in front of the bank to take the rap. You got me out of it. I don't know why, but I'm damned grateful."

"I've heard of you, Laskar. You used to be a big-time bookmaker before you went to prison. You were known throughout the city. They said your word was as good as a gold bond. You were known to payoff a quarter of a million dollars on the races in a single day, without blinking an eye. Your business wasn't exactly legal, but you were an honest bookmaker. Now I find you tied up with a gang of bank robbers. Tell me why!"

Laskar smiled mirthlessly. "Would you believe it, Spider, if I told you I was with them against my will?"

"I'm inclined to believe you. But tell me more."

Laskar leaned forward in his chair. There was no fear or subterfuge in his eyes. He spoke swiftly, his knuckles showing white as he gripped the arms of his chair.

"There's a devil from hell behind all this, Spider. He—he operated on me."

Wentworth's voice was suddenly sharply questioning. "He operated? For what?"

"God knows. When I came out of prison, I was met by a car at the gate. There were two men and a woman in it. The woman was tall and dark, and very beautiful. One of the men I didn't know at all, but the other was Nick Tootsler. I'd taken bets from him when I was making book. He used to be tied up with the rackets—his specialty is the machine gun. They call him Toots around town.

"Well, this Toots told me that he was working for a new boss now, and that his boss wanted to see me, was willing to give me a new start in the bookmaking business, and stake me to a bankroll. I told Toots I didn't need any start. You see, Spider, I had plenty of cash in a safety deposit vault, and it hadn't been touched all the time I was in prison. I figured to take that cash and give up bookmaking altogether. My little girl, Virginia, is seven years old, and I wanted to take her and go to the west coast where they wouldn't know me, and maybe get into some legitimate business. Virginia didn't know her father was in jail. She was only a year old when they arrested me. Her mother died in childbirth, and Virgie has been living with an aunt."

"I see," Wentworth said gently. He was getting a new sidelight on this man. At the time of Laskar's arrest there had been no mention of a child. The bookmaker had no doubt sought to keep his baby daughter out of the sordid mess.

"Go on, Laskar," Wentworth encouraged. "You were saying that Toots and this woman met you in a car."

"Yes. And I told Toots that I didn't need any help. We were right at the prison gate, with the guard looking on, and I knew he couldn't pull any rough stuff. I wasn't having anything to do with him. But that damned woman! She leaned out of the back of the car, and said to me: 'Mr. Laskar, please come and talk to Mr. Tootstler's boss. He has something of interest to show you!' And she took out a little photograph of Virginia."

Wentworth leaned forward, suddenly intensely interested. "A photograph of your daughter?"

"Right. I knew in a minute it was Virgie, because my sister had been sending me pictures all the time I was in jail. The woman said: 'If you will come with us, Mr. Laskar, you will see your daughter. Otherwise you may never see her again!'"

There was suddenly a depth of misery in Laskar's eyes. He spread his hands in a gesture of hopelessness. "What was I to do, Spider?"

"You went with them?"

"I did. They convinced me they had Virginia. I drove down into town with them, and called up my sister on the long distance phone. It was true. Virginia had been missing for two days. The police of our home town couldn't find a single clue. She'd been kidnapped."

CHAPTER 3
THE SPIDER FINDS AN ALLY

BEN LASKAR drew a deep breath, and went on, while a hot fire burned in his eyes. "They blindfolded me, and took me to their boss. They drove around and around, before stopping at their headquarters, so that I lost my sense of direction. The place is a sort of sanatorium, with operating rooms, and private wards that have steel doors and barred windows. They let me look at Virginia through a peephole in a door, and then the boss told me what he wanted of me. He made me give him the key to my safety deposit box, together with a letter authorizing him to remove its contents. That was the price I had to pay to save Virginia—otherwise, he threatened to operate on her and make her an idiot!"

"They let her go?" Wentworth asked.

"Yes. I got that much out of them. I gave them my word I'd sign the letter as soon as Virginia was safe at home again. They knew that Ben Laskar's word is as good as gold, so they agreed. Before I signed I made sure by calling my sister. Then I turned over the key and the letter. Spider, there was over two hundred thousand dollars in cold cash in that box—all my operating capital. I'm broke."

"How did you come to act as their lookout at the Citizens' Bank job?"

"The boss insisted that I promise to work one job with Toots and the gang. He said they wouldn't feel safe unless I was implicated in some crime with them. I agreed—I'd have agreed to anything at the time, when he told me what they'd do to Virgie."

Wentworth leaned forward, spoke with feeling. "Laskar, you've suffered a lot, and I'm going to help you to even up with that gang. Do you want to work with me?"

"Do I!" the bookmaker breathed. "I'm going to devote the rest of my life to paying them back. Why, if it hadn't been for you, I'd be headed right back for jail at this minute. Those devils had it figured out to leave me there from the beginning."

"Did you get a look at this boss of theirs? Do you know his name?"

Laskar shook his head. "All I can tell you is that he's a doctor. They all called him Doc, and he went around dressed like a surgeon, in a white gown. And when he talked to me he wore a white skull cap and an antiseptic mask like the ones they put on when they're operating. All you could see was his eyes. They're black. If I saw those eyes again, I'd know them."

Wentworth remained silent, thoughtful for a while. "What's the name of the man who hit you on the head?"

"Kilter. Sam Kilter. He worked under Toots. I'd like to get him—"

"You don't have to worry about him," Wentworth chuckled. "I gave him a dose of his own medicine—knocked him out, and left him there for the police to find!"

Laskar broke into a wide smile. "Spider, you're tops with me. I wish to Heaven that I wasn't broke and a bum. I'd like to help—"

"You're not going to be broke, Laskar. You're going into business—back in the bookmaking game."

DR. KESTEN

"TOOTS"

LADY STELLA FLOOD

RT. HON. ALBERT FLOOD

Laskar stared into the blinding light, uncomprehendingly. "But it takes money—"

"I'll finance you, Laskar. In the morning, my man will give you two hundred thousand dollars in cash. Go downtown and rent an office, set yourself up the way you used to be. Make your connections, pick up your old Underworld acquaintances. Start taking bets. You will draw a regular salary—from me, and not from the profits. All the profits, if there are any, will go to charity."

"But why—"

"Because I need a man like you to keep in touch with the Underworld. Also, if you're not afraid, I want you to let it be known that anybody who wants to contact the Spider can do so through you. Do you understand?"

"Afraid? Not me, Spider. I'll be your contact man all right.

And I swear to you, Spider, that I'll serve you faithfully."

"I know you will, Laskar. Now I'll have Jackson show you to your room. It'll soon be morning—and there'll be work for you to do!" Wentworth reached across the desk, stretching forth his hand. Laskar took it, and the two men solemnly shook hands.

AS THE bookmaker left the room with Jackson, the telephone on the desk rang. It was connected with the monitor board on the floor below, which was operated by Jenkyns, the butler. There were two quick rings, followed by two slow ones, and Wentworth's blood raced, for he recognized the code. They had established a system of code rings to announce the names of people who phoned often, so that Wentworth generally knew, before picking up the instrument, who was calling.

MORGAN JOHNSON

ANNE HALE

LASKAR

PETER HUMPHRIES

Now, he lifted the French phone, said into the transmitter: "Hello, Nita, dear. I thought you were going to bed when I left you. How come you're still up?"

Nita van Sloan was Richard Wentworth's fiancée—if that term can be applied to a girl who hopes some day to marry a certain man, but wonders at the same time if that marriage will ever come to pass. For though these two loved each other as few men and women love nowadays, they both realized that the peace and happiness of marriage, and the quiet comfort of a home, were not for them as long as the Spider walked the highways and byways of the Underworld. As long as Richard Wentworth pursued his chosen career of crime fighting, as long as he continued to risk his life as he did, Nita van Sloan could not become his wife.

And she loved him well enough to understand that without the risks and the dangers of his present mode of existence, Richard Wentworth would never be the same man. Some day, perhaps, when he had grown older, when the adventurous blood in his veins thinned out, when he had become satiated with the heady scent of the wine of battle and sudden death, he might be ready to come to her arms for the comfort he would need. Until then she was content, if she could not be his wife, to be his constant companion in danger, to share his adventures with him.

It was with Nita that he had been the previous evening, before setting out on that stroll with Apollo, which had led him to the Citizens' Bank & Trust Company. They had gone to a reception and ball tendered by the Right Honorable Albert Flood, former Member of Parliament for the Borough of Axdenster, in England. Flood, an internationally recognized student of economics, had entertained the elite of the city last night, and Richard Wentworth and Nita had been among those invited, as was also Commissioner Stanley Kirkpatrick, the police Commissioner, Wentworth's close friend and tenant.

Flood had taken the opportunity of speaking in private with Commissioner Kirkpatrick concerning his sister, Lady Stella Flood, who had disappeared the day after their arrival from England, and of whom there had so far been no trace, in spite of diligent quest by the police.

Wentworth had been present at that interview, by reason of his friendship for the commissioner, and also because he had been careful to build up for himself a reputation as a dilettante criminologist. Wentworth had promised his help in the matter of finding the Lady Stella Flood, who, her brother was certain, was not dead. The reason for that certainty on his part was the fact that she had left a note in her room, stating that for personal reasons she found it necessary to go away for a while, and for her brother not to worry about her.

It was this problem that had been occupying Wentworth's mind on the way home from the reception, so that after he had seen Nita safely in her apartment, he had taken Apollo for a stroll.

Nita's voice sounded strangely perturbed on the telephone. "Dick!" she exclaimed. "I couldn't get to sleep. You know how I experience premonitions of danger. Well, I was almost sure you were in trouble. I—I've been awake for an hour now, trying to get up courage enough to phone you—I knew you'd laugh at me if I woke you up with my silly fears."

Wentworth essayed a laugh. "Well, Nita, you see I'm at home all right. I won't laugh at you, if you'll promise to go back to bed—"

"No, no, Dick, you can't fool me. Something is the trouble; otherwise, why would Jenkyns be up at this hour? He couldn't have been asleep, because he answered the phone on the first ring."

"Nita, dear, you're turning out to be a regular detective. I'll have to tell Jenkyns to sleep a little more soundly next time—"

"Dick! You can't laugh it off like that. Something's up. Tell me—has it anything to do with the Citizens' Bank robbery?"

"How do you know about that?" he asked sharply.

"I had the radio going while I sat up, and I caught the police broadcast. And now I've tuned in on WNOS, the twenty-four hour station, and they're broadcasting a Radio News Bulletin on it." Her voice became vibrant with excitement. "I was right. You're in something up to your neck, Dick. And you're not going to keep me out of it. *I'm coming over, Mr. Wentworth!*"

"No, no, Nita!" he cried softly into the transmitter. "Stay out of this—"

But she had already hung up. Wentworth smiled ruefully. He might have known that it would be useless to try to keep Nita van Sloan out of anything that promised excitement. And he loved her for it.

HE CRADLED the phone, and swung around to the small, compact radio which rested on a shelf behind him, tuned in on

WNOS. He was just in time to catch part of the news bulletin on the Citizens' Bank affair:

> "... that there was apparently some falling-out among the bandits after the robbery, for one of their number was found unconscious, with a fractured jaw,

on the sidewalk before the bank building. An abandoned car with the right rear tire punctured by a bullet had been reported found two blocks from Fifth Avenue. The body of the car was dented by thirty-eight calibre slugs, apparently fired by two automatics.

"The unconscious man with the fractured jaw has been identified as Sam Kilter, a gangster with a long criminal record, but who has never gone in for bank robbery before.

"It is a mystery to the police how the sedan's tire could have been punctured, for Kilter must have been knocked out before the car started away. Commissioner Kirkpatrick, who was aroused from bed to take direct charge of the investigation, expressed the opinion that there must have been at least one other person on the sidewalk with Kilter when the sedan fled. Every possible facility of the Department is being used to trace that person...."

Wentworth smiled to himself. Kirkpatrick was no fool. He would guess much more than he gave out for publication. Down at the ballistics bureau there were plenty of slugs which the police had preserved, and which they knew to have been fired from the twin automatics of the Spider. Kirkpatrick would compare those slugs with the ones found in the street—and he would know who that "other person" was.

The Commissioner was morally certain that Richard Wentworth and the Spider were one and the same; but he lacked proof. And though he was Wentworth's close friend, he had often assured him that if he could prove that Wentworth was the Spider, he would personally make the arrest.

Wentworth picked up the phone, asked for Jackson. "See that my two automatics are well hidden, Jackson," he ordered. "And replace them in my room with two others. We may have a visitor soon."

The Radio News Bulletin was continuing, with the announcer's voice growing more excited as he related the thrilling incidents of the morning:

"… Commissioner Kirkpatrick has already ordered one arrest in this case—that of Josiah Stryker, the night watchman of the bank. Stryker's story was so weird and unreasonable that no credence is being placed in it, and Stryker is held as an accomplice. The front doors of the bank had not been forced or blown open. They were found to have been opened from within, and the burglar alarm switch was pulled off.

"When questioned, Stryker stated he had been summoned to the front door by the ringing of the night bell, and had seen Morgan Johnson, president of the bank, standing outside. Johnson motioned to him to open up, according to the night watchman, and Stryker did so, first turning off the burglar alarm so as not to cause it to ring in the offices of the Bankers' Protective Association, to which the wires were hooked up.

"Immediately upon entering, Johnson, according to the night watchman, struck Stryker with a blackjack which he had held concealed in the palm of his hand. Stryker declares that is all he knows.

"Commissioner Kirkpatrick found that at the time of the robbery, Morgan Johnson was at home in bed, having returned more than an hour before from a reception given by the Right Honorable Albert Flood. Stryker was therefore placed under arrest.

"It will be recalled that Morgan Johnson was the victim of a kidnapping plot, and...."

Wentworth allowed the announcer's voice to trail off while his own thoughts sped from point to point of the problem. Now he was breathing quickly, like a bloodhound on the scent. His hands were clenched at his sides, and there was sweat on his forehead from the effort at concentration to which he was forcing himself. Some simple thing was the key to this mystery—of that he was sure. But that simple key eluded him somehow. If he could only put his finger....

HE WAS so lost in concentration that he did not hear the outside doorbell ring. A few moments later, Nita van Sloan knocked at the door and entered. He had turned off the glaring desk light, and now the room was illuminated by a pleasant, indirect lighting system that set off Nita's slender beauty to perfection. She was flushed, vivid, full of vitality and suppressed excitement.

51

Apollo, who enjoyed the freedom of the house, ambled in after her, stood looking up at her with tongue hanging, as if he, too, wished to express his appreciation of her vibrant beauty.

Wentworth got up from behind the desk, came around and took her in his arms. Her soft body nestled against his for a long sweet moment, as their lips met in a swift kiss.

Nita was the first to push away. "Dick!" she chided. "You shouldn't have tried to fool me over the phone. I have a right—"

"Yes, I know, dear. But this looks as if it may be more danger-ous than anything I've tackled. I hope—"

"To keep me out of it. Well, you won't. And I've got some-thing important for you. But I won't tell unless you promise that I'm in on this—"

"I promise," he groaned. "Now, what's the news?"

"The Right Honorable Albert Flood, our host of last evening—is dead!"

"What!"

She nodded. "Murdered. After I talked to you on the phone, I discovered that I didn't have my bag. I thought I had forgot-ten it at the reception, and I didn't want every Tom, Dick and Harry looking into it. It has my pistol, and a few other things that I'd rather were not seen. So I phoned, knowing that the servants would still be up, clearing away. Well, the phone was answered by a detective. After I gave him my name, he told me who he was, and began asking questions. He wanted to know where I'd been for the last hour. I refused to answer unless he'd tell me the reason for his questions, and then he gave me the bad news—after the last of the guests left, the host put on his coat, and went out, saying he needed a breath of air. Twenty minutes later, the patrolman on the beat discovered his dead body, shot twice through the heart, in an alley in the next block!"

Wentworth whistled. "They suspect you, Nita?"

She shrugged. "I don't know, Dick, but I'm afraid so. The detective—Detective Chalmers, he said he was—asked me if I owned a twenty-two calibre pistol, and I had to admit it, because it was right there in my bag. Then Chalmers said: 'You stay right where you are, young woman—we're calling for you. Want to ask you a few questions.' I waited a few moments, intending to call you, but I looked out of the window, and saw a radio car pulling up outside the house. Now, if they wanted to ask me questions, they wouldn't have rushed a radio car there, would they?"

Wentworth was worried. "This complicates things, Nita. Of course, you can prove that you were home—"

He paused as the phone rang. It was Jenkyns. "Commissioner Kirkpatrick is here, sir," the butler announced, "and insists on seeing you at once. He wants to go upstairs—"

"No!" Wentworth said sharply. "I'll come down."

"He has two men with him, sir—"

"Is Jackson there?"

"Yes, sir."

"Give him the sign to shut the steel gate at the foot of the stairs."

"I've already done that, sir," Jenkyns said smugly. "The gate is shut. That is why Commissioner Kirkpatrick was good enough to remain below until I phoned you."

"Good men!" Wentworth said warmly. "Hold the fort. I'll be right down."

He swung to Nita. "It's Kirkpatrick, with a couple of men. I was expecting this call." In as few words as possible he related to her the events of the morning. "Kirk may be here about those slugs, which he must have checked with the Spider's by this time, or else he may be calling about the business at Albert Flood's. I don't think it's the latter, because he'd hardly have had time to get around to that. Anyway, I don't want him to find you here. No matter what happens, don't come down unless I phone up that the coast is clear."

She nodded, and stood with her hand on Apollo's head, watching Wentworth go down the long corridor to the staircase that led into the lower apartment.

CHAPTER 4
A GATE MADE OF PAPER

COMING DOWN the stairs, Wentworth could see past the iron-grilled gate that dropped from the ceiling, effectively barring entrance to the floor above. It was one of the protective measures he had built into the apartment. It could be operated from any one of four spots throughout the place.

On the other side of the gate, Commissioner Kirkpatrick, flanked by two plainclothes men, was fuming and fretting, shouting at old Jenkyns who merely listened to him in stony silence.

Wentworth smiled, approaching the gate unnoticed. He

pressed a button, and the gate rose quickly. He stepped under it before it was half way up, then placed his foot upon a board in the floor of the foyer, close to the wall. At once the gate began to descend.

At that moment Kirkpatrick turned, saw him and the moving gate, and uttered an exclamation of anger. He rushed toward Wentworth, shouting: "Let me upstairs—"

He stopped, frustrated. The gate was all the way down again.

Wentworth said suavely: "So sorry, Kirk. If I had only known you wanted to go up, I might have held the gate open. Of course, you have a perfect right to come rushing into a friend's house at four in the morning and demand to enter his private quarters. I understand policemen always act like this."

Kirkpatrick restrained himself with a visible effort, attempted to keep cool. He knew Wentworth well, and he knew that Wentworth's sharp wit would always enrage him, while Wentworth himself remained as cool as a cucumber. Time and again he had promised himself never to lose his temper with this man. They were friends, yes. But there was always between them that latent suspicion within Kirkpatrick's mind that his friend was also the Spider.

Jenkyns broke in to say: "I was just apologizing, sir, to Commissioner Kirkpatrick, for not being able to allow him upstairs. I explained that it was rather unusual—"

Kirkpatrick had mastered himself by this time. He was a handsome, florid man in his late forties, with an air of dignity and authority acquired from long years of command.

He forced a smile, said to Wentworth, "I'm sorry if I seemed to act hastily, Dick. The fact of the matter is—"his voice took on a slightly sarcastic tinge—"I wanted your advice upon a certain subject, and I was so eager to see you, I couldn't wait. As an old friend of yours, I thought it would be perfectly all right for me to go right upstairs. Imagine my surprise when I was confronted with this beastly gate—"

"No doubt," Wentworth said drily, "you wanted to introduce me to these two worthy gentlemen who are with you? Perhaps you wished to suggest a little game of pinochle—"

"No, Dick, they're working on a case with me. You've heard of the robbery of the Citizens' Bank & Trust Company?"

Wentworth raised his eyebrows. "Robbery? I'm sorry, Kirk, but I haven't seen a newspaper—"

"This happened too recently to be in the paper. I thought perhaps—you—*might have witnessed it!*"

"Me—witness a robbery? What makes you think so?"

"Oh, nothing much. By the way, Dick, would you mind if I took a look at your guns—you know, the ones you were carrying tonight."

"Was I carrying guns tonight?"

"You certainly were. I could see the bulge under your armpits—"

"You mean at Albert Flood's reception?"

"Y-yes. That's right. That's where I saw the bulge—"

Wentworth grinned. "Try again, Kirk. You know very well that it's impossible to wear shoulder holsters with evening clothes. And you also know that if you'd seen that bulge, you would have insisted on examining the guns, the way you always

56

do with me. However—" as he saw the discomfited look in the Commissioner's face—"for your benefit, I'll tell you that I did have a gun or two in my overcoat pocket, which I handed to the man at the door. Had you looked in my overcoat, you might have found them there."

Kirkpatrick said coldly: "May I see those guns?"

"Of course." Wentworth motioned to Jenkyns, "Will you kindly bring my guns here so that the Commissioner may examine them?"

Jenkyns bowed and went to get them. In a few moments he returned with a pair of automatics.

KIRKPATRICK EXAMINED them closely, sniffed at the barrels, removed the clips. His hands had gotten full of oil in the process. He looked up, frowned at Jenkyns. "Did you just oil these guns?"

"No, sir," the butler said imperturbably. "Those guns were oiled more than a week ago."

Kirkpatrick grunted. "So you say." He glanced up at Wentworth. "It's possible, Dick, that these guns were used tonight, and then cleaned and oiled, isn't it?"

"Quite right, Kirk. Where would you say they'd been used?"

"At the Citizens' Bank & Trust Company robbery. You know as well as I do that the Citizens' was robbed a little more than an hour ago. A number of shots were fired, and I'm sure there was one more person at the scene of the crime than has been accounted for. Now these guns—we could check them down at Ballistics—"

Wentworth smiled. "You may rest assured, Kirk, that neither

of those guns was fired tonight." His eyes met those of the Commissioner, and slowly, Kirkpatrick handed the two automatics back to Jenkyns. It was like a game of chess. Kirkpatrick knew that Wentworth would make no statement other than the truth. Wentworth had called "check," and the Commissioner hastened to move out of that position, to adopt another.

"Will you also give me your word, Dick, that you weren't present at the robbery of that bank this morning?"

Wentworth's lips tightened. "You have no right to ask me that, Kirk. I resent it. Why don't you go around asking the six million other inhabitants of New York the same thing? Why pick on me?"

"You haven't answered me yet," Kirkpatrick pointed out.

"I don't intend to."

"Then, regretfully, I shall have to insist on going through your premises."

"Out of the question. Let me point out to you, Kirk, that a man's home is his castle under our law—"

"Not," Kirkpatrick broke in gently, "under all conditions. For instance, when an officer holds a search warrant, then a man's home ceases to be his castle!"

"You have a search warrant?" Wentworth demanded incredulously.

"Here. Read it for yourself. I awoke a County Judge to get it. You see, Dick, if my suspicions are unfounded, then I want to know it. Let's put our cards on the table. You've known for a long time that I suspect you of being the Spider. I've never been absolutely positive, though, and believe me, I've prayed that it might not be so, for I value our friendship highly. But you know me well enough to understand that if you *are* the Spider, you need expect no mercy from me."

"So you want to convince yourself either way—"

"And be done once and for all with this miserable suspicion!"

"Very estimable of you, I'm sure," Wentworth murmured. Suddenly he raised his voice. *"Did you get it all, Jackson?"*

From the rear of the apartment came Jackson's voice. "I got it, sir!"

"You know what to do?"

"Yes, sir!"

"Then go ahead!"

Kirkpatrick stared at Wentworth, puzzled. He swung on his two men. "Go get that fellow Jackson! Don't let him leave!"

The two men saluted, raced through to the rear of the apartment.

"They might have saved their efforts, Kirk," Wentworth said, smiling. "Jackson is gone."

"But how? There's only one door leading to the roof—"

Suddenly he stopped, scowling, as the two officers returned. One of them reported: "He must have got away, sir. There's a private elevator door in the rear. We couldn't get the door open, but that's the way he must have gone."

"All right," Kirkpatrick growled, "never mind him. Let's get on with the search." He stuffed the search warrant in his pocket, moved over toward Wentworth threateningly. "Open that gate for me, Dick, or I shall be obliged to place you under arrest, and cut the gate open with an acetylene torch!"

Wentworth stalled. "What do you expect to find up there, Kirk?"

"For one thing, maybe I'll find the guns that you really carried tonight." He smiled twistedly. "You don't think you fooled me with those ringers, do you? I know you've got permits from every county in the state. You must own fifty different kinds of firearms."

"I suppose I do. But you can take my word for it that you won't find any guns upstairs that were used tonight."

"Well, maybe I'll find something else."

"For instance?"

"For instance—maybe I'll find Nita van Sloan!"

Wentworth grew cold. "What do you want of her?"

"You know it already, Dick, but I don't mind telling you again, for the sake of the record. The Right Honorable Albert Flood was murdered outside his home this morning. He was shot twice through the heart with a twenty-two calibre gun. The gun was found not far from the body. It was in a lady's handbag. We checked the gun's number, and we examined the bag. *Both of them belong to Nita van Sloan!*"

THIS WAS what Wentworth had feared. The force of that announcement struck him like a sledge-hammer. Nita had been at home alone; she would not be able to prove a convincing alibi. The force of circumstantial evidence was against her. The only thing lacking was a motive, and a clever prosecuting attorney could always dig up a motive of some sort.

It would mean that Nita would have to spend months in jail awaiting trial. He never doubted for a moment that she was innocent. But no one can tell what will happen at a murder trial. Murder jurors are somehow different from other jurors. And Nita's life would hang upon the judgment of twelve men. She herself would be helpless in a cell, unable to move in her own defense.

Steadily he faced Kirkpatrick. "Do you believe," he asked slowly, "that Nita murdered Albert Flood?"

Kirkpatrick lowered his eyes. "It doesn't matter what I believe," he muttered. "I'm a policeman, and I must do my duty as I see it. I must arrest that person toward whom the evidence points—even if it be you, Dick, or Nita!"

"But—"

Kirkpatrick waved him aside. "Stop stalling, Dick. Now I'm sure she's up there. You open that gate, or I'll have it burned through. I've got an emergency squad downstairs, with an acetylene torch—"

"Let me read that search warrant," Wentworth said desperately.

The Commissioner shrugged. "You're entitled to that. But don't take too long reading it. I'll give you five minutes!"

Wentworth took the document which the other handed to him, and inspected it carefully. It was entirely in order, and signed by a judge of the County Court, authorizing the Commissioner of Police of the City of New York to enter "peaceably or by force as the occasion may require, into the premises of one, Richard Wentworth, etc... etc...."

Kirkpatrick said bitingly: "There's nothing the matter with that warrant, Dick. It's all shipshape, and in order. Come on.

Your time's expired, and we're going up. Will you raise the gate, or—"

He stopped, staring in amazement at Wentworth, who was smiling at him broadly.

"What—"

"Sorry, Kirk, but you're not going up!"

The Commissioner and his two men gaped at Jackson, who had just reappeared from the rear of the apartment, accompanied by an elderly, gray-haired man, clad in pajamas over which he had thrown an overcoat. The gray-haired man held a paper in his hand, and was smiling thinly.

Wentworth said to Kirkpatrick: "Of course, you know Mr. Martin Abercombie, my attorney? He's a neighbor of ours—lives on the third floor."

"Of course I know him. How do you do, Abercombie?"

Martin Abercombie, whose reputation as an attorney yielded to none, was the president of the Bar Association, and Wentworth's personal lawyer. He nodded to Kirkpatrick, advanced smiling, and handed the paper to Wentworth.

"This is going to cost you plenty of money, Mr. Wentworth," he said. "I don't get up in the middle of the night for everybody!"

"Make the bill as steep as you like, Abercombie," Wentworth told him. "It'll be worth every penny—to see the look on Kirk's face when he reads this!" With a flourish he handed the paper over.

The Commissioner frowned down at it. "What—what's this?"

"This, my dear Commissioner, is what Jackson went to get. I've been expecting you to try a search warrant on me, and I've had a standing arrangement. When you announced that you had the warrant, Jackson left immediately and went down to the third floor, where he got Mr. Abercombie out of bed. Then they both went up to the twelfth floor, and awoke Judge Collings by, of the Court of General Sessions, and he signed the paper I have just given you. That paper, as you can see, is an injunction order, restraining you from exercising your search warrant, until such time as Judge Collings by may hear argument on a motion to vacate the warrant entirely!"

Slowly, as Kirkpatrick realized that he was beaten at his own game, his face flushed a dull red. But he was a sportsman. He smiled, extended his hand to Wentworth.

"No hard feelings, Dick. This is perfectly legal, and as long as you confine yourself to legal procedure, I have no complaint against you. In a way, perhaps I'm glad that I don't have to go upstairs. You can't tell what I might find!"

Smilingly, Wentworth conducted them all to the door, saw them across the lawn and into the elevator. Then he returned to the apartment, but he was no longer smiling.

HIS ORDERS rapped out with the staccato rattle of machine gun fire. "Jenkyns! Jackson! We've got to act quickly now. Kirkpatrick isn't giving up as easy as all that. He'll be back. You, Jenkyns, open that gate, go up and get Miss van Sloan out of here. Be sure you remove every sign of her presence. Jackson, do the same for Ben Laskar. Clear the house of every trace of them!"

Wentworth himself got his coat and hat, picked a sword cane out from among the selection in the rack in the hall, and saw to it that the two automatics were fully loaded.

"Tell Miss van Sloan to go to the Marion Hotel and register under the name of Irene Rogers. Tell Laskar to go to the Franklin Hotel, and use the name of Zachary Smith. I'll contact them both in the morning. You, Jackson, go to the banks where you hold my power of attorney, and draw two hundred thousand dollars in large bills. Take the money to Laskar. You can give it to him without a receipt. Both of you will return here, and when Ram Singh comes back, I will expect the three of you to wait for my orders. I shall be needing you all before the day is over, if I've sized things up right!"

He stopped on his way to the private elevator, called back: "Jackson, there's one more chore for you to do—feed and groom that horse in garage number three. Beg, borrow or steal some feed, but have that horse ready for me. I'm going to use the milk wagon tonight!"

Jackson saluted snappily. "Your orders noted, sir!" he said.

Wentworth smiled at both faithful servants, and stepped into the private elevator, descended to the basement. There, he made his way into garage number four, where a nondescript car of ancient vintage was parked. This car was just ordinary enough so that it could be driven anywhere without attracting attention; but anyone glancing under the hood would have been surprised at the perfect condition of the motor. That motor was of the latest design, capable of delivering all the power necessary to run away from the fastest cars on the road.

Wentworth pressed a button, and the rear door of the garage opened. He drove out into the alley alongside the church, and as the car passed a certain spot in the alley it intercepted a photo-electric ray which automatically closed the door. Wentworth drove out into the street, then around the block, passing in front of his apartment house. He smiled and nodded as he noted the figures of two men at the corner, who were unmistakably policemen. On the other side of the street a police car was parked at the curb, with a man at the wheel, his eyes glued to the front of the Hopecrest Apartments.

Kirkpatrick had lost no time in posting his guards. But they would have a long and unrewarded vigil, for no one from Wentworth's apartment was going to use the front entrance today. No doubt there was also a police shadow posted somewhere in the back courtyard, between the garages and the rear of the house, but that shadow would see no one, for Jenkyns and Jackson would use the basement passage to the garages in leaving and entering.

Wentworth drove around the block once more, then turned into Central Park West and headed south. He stopped once at a drug store to look up the address of Douglas Fenner, the producer of "Spanish Afternoon," in which Anne Hale acted the star role. Fenner had published an appeal to the Spider for help in locating Anne Hale, and the Spider was going to interview him.

But first, Wentworth stopped at the home of Mike Fogarty, a private detective in whom he placed the utmost confidence. After rousing Fogarty out of bed and ordering him to go into the bathroom and splash some cold water on his face to wake himself up, Wentworth gave him swift instructions.

"Here's what I want, Mike. Somewhere in this city, there's a private sanatorium or hospital where some kind of devil's work is going on. I suspect it's the headquarters of the gang that has been doing most of the kidnapping jobs in the last few months. The place is run by a man who is known only as 'Doc.' I want to find that place."

Fogarty rubbed the sleep from his eyes. He was a big man, with a great, hanging paunch, and a double chin, and he was well on in the forties. Such of his hair as was left at the fringes of his scalp indicated that he had once been red-headed. His pajama coat hung from his great shoulders like a sack, and he was busy lighting a cigar with one hand while he held up his pajama trousers with the other.

He finally got the cigar lit, and threw a quizzical glance at Wentworth. "Is that all you want of me, Mr. Wentworth? All you want is that I should find a sanatorium that's run by a guy called Doc! Why don't you ask me to find a restaurant that's run by a Greek? That might be easier!"

"Never mind the wisecracks, Fogarty!" Wentworth snapped. "I don't care how many men you put on this, and I don't care how big an expense account you run up. *I want that information by noon!*"

Fogarty looked dubious. "Okay, but I don't guarantee results. I might dig up twenty joints like the one you mention. Will I go in to each of them and ask has there been any shenanigans going on around there recently?"

"I've got more of a lead for you, Mike. The right hand man of this 'Doc' is a gunman named Nick Tootsler—Toots for short."

Fogarty fairly leaped from his chair, "Now you're talking,

Mr. Wentworth. Do I know Toots! That punk gets coked up, and he'll go gunning for the whole United States Navy! I know just where Toots hangs out. He's got a certain lady friend on Columbus Avenue, and if I put a couple of shadows on her house, they'll be able to pick him up in no time, and follow him to this here sanatorium!"

"I don't want to depend on that alone, Mike," Wentworth said seriously. "I want you also to put out as many investigators as you need, to dig into every sanatorium in the city and report anything that may look queer. It's damned important, Mike!"

Fogarty looked at him queerly. "Just how important is it, Mr. Wentworth?"

"Important enough for me to pay you two thousand dollars if you get me the information by noon!"

"It's something big?"

Wentworth nodded. "Big—and dangerous. Tell your men to be careful. If one of them finds the right place, and he's spotted, his life will be in danger."

"You don't need to tell me that, Mr. Wentworth. If the guys that handled those kidnappings are holing out in this here sanatorium, they won't let a little killing stand in their way."

Wentworth started for the door. "I'm depending on you. If you get the information, don't phone me at my apartment—my wire may be tapped. Call the Marion Hotel, and ask for Miss Irene Rogers. Make your report to her, and it'll get to me!"

He shook hands with Fogarty, and went down to his car. He delayed only long enough to make sure that certain objects within the car were easily accessible. Those objects consisted of a cape, a wide-brimmed hat, and a compact box of make-up materials. With the aid of this paraphernalia, Wentworth would be able to assume the disguise of the Spider, the disguise that was so familiar to the Underworld. It was as the Spider that he intended to interview Douglas Fenner. Swiftly he headed his car across the Queensboro Bridge toward Fenner's residence....

CHAPTER 5
THE LEPER APPEARS

THE HOME of Douglas Fenner was a pretty little Colonial house, set well back from the road, with enough grounds on either side to justify his having come to Long Island to live.

Wentworth had asked directions at the little town on the Merrick Road, about a mile back, so that now he recognized the place at once, and turned in from the highway. He could see that the lights of the residence were all on, which was strange, considering that it was still only five o'clock in the morning. The late winter sun had not risen, and it might have been midnight for the pitch darkness which surrounded the place.

As soon as he had swung his car into the driveway, Wentworth knew that he had come in time for trouble. There was another car, facing him, which had apparently been backed into the driveway, with its lights out.

Beside the car, two men were lifting a third man out of the auto, while a woman sat at the wheel. Under the glare of his headlights, Wentworth recognized that woman. It was the same one who had driven the getaway car at the Citizens' Bank & Trust Company robbery!

There was evidently no attempt being made at concealment by the occupants of the parked car, for the man who was being carried out of the car was shouting hoarsely for help, and the residents of the house had already been alarmed. The front door was open, and framed in the doorway stood a man in a bathrobe, holding a large revolver in a shaky hand. Behind him stood a woman, who had hastily thrown a kimono over her nightgown.

Wentworth could see the scene distinctly in his headlights, and the faces and hands of the gunmen who were lifting out the third man were clearly visible. Neither was the same as the ones who had participated in the bank robbery. They both wore gloves. The face of the man they were lifting out was also sharply etched in the light, and Wentworth shuddered at sight of the splotchy patches on his cheeks, and the scabs under his eyes. In spite of those patches and scabs, he recognized the man at once, and a cold shudder ran through his frame.

He acted even as the scene registered upon his brain. He had already changed to the cape and hat of the Spider, and had changed the appearance of his face with the aid of the plastic material and nose plates in his make-up box. He was, to all intents and purposes, the Spider.

And it was the Spider that leaped from the car like an avenging angel, both automatics spitting lead at the two gunmen.

They had both dropped their burden at the approach of Wentworth's car and the man with the splotchy face screamed, rolled over and over, away from the line of fire. The gunmen had been holding automatics even while they carried their man, and their first shots were directed at the headlights, even before Wentworth had leaped to the ground. Their first volley blasted both lights into oblivion, flinging the grounds into darkness except for the light that streamed from the open door of the house.

At the same time, the woman in the gunmen's sedan switched on her own headlights, bathing the Spider in the powerful glare. His caped figure was sharply limned in the twin beams, and the gunmen uttered shouts of dismay.

"The Spider! It's the Spider! *God!*"

Their shouts of consternation were drowned by the deep-throated roar of the Spider's heavy automatics, mingling with the explosions of their own guns. The night was violated with screaming lead and whining slugs that whistled their grim messages of death. The two gunmen were shooting at a clearly visible mark, but they were shooting hastily, with panic in their hearts. The Spider, on the other hand, shot coolly, deliberately, his targets virtually hidden from him by the glare of the headlights in his face.

Yet he disdained to shoot out those headlights. He fired at the flashes of the gunmen's own automatics, aiming on a level with the flashes and a little to the right. He knew that men shooting like this in a gunfight would hold their guns straight out ahead of them, and by aiming as he did he expected to strike them in the heart.

This was not the first time the Spider had engaged in fights like this, where the odds seemed all against him. And the Spider was still alive to fight again, while those antagonists who had dared to trade shots with him were in their graves.

The two thugs knew that, and hopeless fear assailed their hearts only a moment before Wentworth's searching slugs smashed them backward into death and oblivion.

The fight had been swift and intense. Its entire duration was less than a minute. And even before the firing ceased, the woman in the gangster's car stepped down hard on the accelerator, shifted into first and raced across the grounds, leaving the road to avoid Wentworth's car, and fled, deserting her two dead accomplices.

AS HER sedan roared in a wide, mad turn into the highway, the Spider swung, bleak-eyed after it, raised his automatics. But he did not pull the triggers. Subconsciously he had counted his shots—nine from each gun, a full clip. It had been necessary to use that many shots, for he was shooting blind. Now there were none left for the fleeing woman.

He shrugged as the sedan disappeared down the highway, headed back toward New York. He would have liked to talk to that woman, if he got the chance. His first impression had been that she was not the type to associate with killers, and he still clung to that impression. He was not sorry that his clips were empty.

Now that the grounds were in darkness again, he could see the man and the woman in the doorway of the house, cowering on their own threshold. That would be Mr. and Mrs. Douglas Fenner. He started toward them, inserting fresh clips in his guns as he walked. And suddenly he heard a choked groan from almost at his feet, and remembered the struggling man the gunmen had been lifting out of the car.

He produced his fountain-pen flashlight, turned it downwards, and gasped. He had been right in his identification, had recognized this man at first glance. It was Doctor Peter Humphries, the head of the National Research Clinic. Humphries, a very wealthy man in his own right, had been one of those kidnapped along with Morgan Johnson and Anne Hale. Here he was back again, as Johnson had come back. But there was very evidently something radically wrong with him.

Humphries was groaning, getting to his knees. His face was ugly to behold under the flashlight, blotched and scaly, and there were the same blotches on the backs of his hands.

Fenner had gotten up enough courage to come off the porch now, and Wentworth called to him: "Have no fear. Come closer. I am the Spider, to whom you appealed in the newspapers. If you wish to speak with me do so quickly. The police from the town will be here soon!"

Fenner exclaimed eagerly: "Yes, yes! The Spider! God! I'm glad you came. I thought it was you, when these men pulled up in the car. I opened the door, and there they were, struggling with this poor man—"

He bent down to lend a hand to Humphries, who was still struggling to get to his knees, though he was apparently not wounded. But before Fenner could put a hand on Humphries, Wentworth exclaimed sharply:

"Don't touch him!"

Fenner, startled, drew back sharply. "W-why—"

The Spider leaped from the car like an avenging angel.

Peter Humphries, on the ground, laughed harshly. "So you know—what's the matter with me Spider!"

Slowly, almost compassionately, Wentworth said: "Leprosy?"

"Yes."

"But—you seem to have it in the advanced stage. You didn't have it before you were kidnapped?"

"No. I'm a doctor. I know as well as you do, that it's impossible to have leprosy in this stage after only three months. But by God, that's what I have! They operated on me. But there's no way known to science that they could have given me this. It's— some sort of black magic!"

Until the last sentence, Humphries' words had been almost those of a clinician, speaking impersonally of some patient's case. But suddenly his voice broke, and he sobbed: "I'm a pariah, now! A pariah!"

He lifted a shaky, scaly forefinger, and pointed it at Fenner. "Look out they don't do the same to you, by God! Read that letter!" And he fell forward on the ground, unconscious.

Tremblingly, Fenner bent and picked up a white square of paper at his feet.

IT WAS a sealed envelope. His fingers shook as he turned it over, read his own name written on it. His hands were trembling so that he could not open it, and Wentworth took it from him, tore the edge, and carefully withdrew the single sheet of paper within, handling it gingerly so as not to disturb any fingerprints that might be on it.

While Mrs. Fenner remained cowering in the doorway,

Wentworth read the strange letter, holding his flashlight on it while Fenner peered over his shoulder:

Douglas Fenner:

Do you believe it impossible to give a man a ten-year developed case of leprosy? Well, look at Humphries. We are delivering him to you, solely as an example of what will happen to you if you persist in seeking the help of the Spider. Do nothing, send the Spider away when he comes, and nothing will happen to you. Anne Hale is none of your concern. You have a good understudy in her part, and you're not losing anything. Don't be a fool and yield to sentiment. Forget about Anne Hale, forget about the Spider. Or would you like your wife to see you the way Humphries is now?

DOC.

The letter was written in a careful, meticulous longhand, and almost before they were finished with it, the writing began to fade from the paper!

Wentworth swore under his breath. "Doc," whoever he might be, was very clever in addition to being a good scientist. He had used the same kind of ink which the Intelligence and Espionage departments of most nations had employed during the World War—an ink that disappeared as soon as it was exposed to the decomposing powers of the oxygen in the air.

Nevertheless, Wentworth carefully folded the now blank sheet of paper, and put it in his pocket. He swung on Fenner.

"Quick! Before the police get here! You wanted to get in touch with me, and here I am. You have something important to tell me about the whereabouts of Anne Hale? You said that if I'd come, you could tell me enough to interest me in her case?"

Fenner was staring up at him now, as if he were a ghost. His lips were trembling, and a film of perspiration covered his forehead and lay almost in pools in the little puckers under his eyes.

"N-no, no!" he quavered. "I won't say a thing. Look! Look at Humphries! God, I don't want anything like that to happen to me!"

Humphries was lying still at their feet, but the breath was coming from him in wheezing gasps.

Wentworth seized Fenner by the collar of his pajamas. "Look here, man you've *got* to talk. It's not only Anne Hale, it's dozens of other innocent men and women who've disappeared in the last few months. You said in your advertisement that you loved Anne Hale like a daughter, that you'd do anything for her. Well, now is your chance—"

"No, no! I don't want anything to do with it. I won't talk, I tell you! Go away, please. I—I'm not an adventurous man. I—I didn't think it would be anything like this. Leprosy! God!"

Wentworth scowled. There was little time. He could hear a siren screaming on the highway now, perhaps a mile away. He gave up the attempt to make the frightened Fenner talk, pushed him aside and bent swiftly next to Humphries.

"Humphries," he said speaking swiftly against time, "do you know who did this to you?"

Humphries, still lying on his face, shook his head. His hands were twisting at the envelope in which Fenner's letter had come, and which Wentworth had dropped to the ground. Wentworth pulled the envelope out of his hands.

"Look here, Humphries, can you give me any clue to the people who made you a leper? Can you give me a clue to 'Doc?'"

Again Humphries shook his head. "I don't know a thing, except that they kept feeding me ether, and operating on me. My body is covered with scars—"

Wentworth couldn't wait. The police siren was drawing too near for comfort. He left in the middle of Humphries' sentence, leaped into his car, backed swiftly out into the highway, turning on his cowl lights to replace the headlights that had been shot out. He made a complete turn, and drove toward the town, passing the racing police car on its way to Fenner's home.

The Spider's face was still bleak and grim as he drove back to New York. So far, he told himself he had accomplished nothing—nothing....

COMMISSIONER KIRKPATRICK crashed his fist down on the glass top of his desk, and glared at the semi-circle of police officials gathered in his office.

There were four deputy commissioners and six inspectors in the room, comprising the executive personnel of the Department.

"Gentlemen," Kirkpatrick boomed, "the Mayor demands action; the press demands action. The public demands action. It's up to us to give 'em action!"

The men facing him shifted uncomfortably, and glanced at each other. Before anyone of them could speak, Kirkpatrick went on.

"All these things tie into one case somehow—of that I'm sure. But our object is twofold. First, we've got to break up and capture the gang that's behind all these kidnappings that have disgraced the city in the last few months; and I'll swear it's the same gang that's responsible for the Citizens' Bank Robbery. Secondly, we've got to get the Spider. He's made a fool of us long enough."

Inspector McCrorty, an old-timer on the force, grinned and asked: "How we going to get the Spider, sir? We've been trying for a long time now. I hear tell you even made another try early this morning!"

McCrorty was an inspector of such long standing that he dared to say things the others would not have dared to utter. Kirkpatrick flushed at the thought of how he had been outwitted by Wentworth that morning, at the Hopecrest Apartments. It was almost noon now, and his watchers reported that neither Wentworth nor his servants, nor Nita van Sloan, had been seen to leave the building. Yet he was sure that Wentworth was out— had gotten out somehow. He had received a report of the events at Fenner's home, and he knew that the Spider had been abroad that morning.

He waved his hand impatiently at McCrorty's comment. "Never mind that, Mac. I have my own plans for trapping the Spider. Right now we'll concentrate on this gang. Let's see how they stand. So far, they've scored a hundred percent, and we've scored zero.

"Anne Hale is still missing. So are a dozen others, among them some of our great artists, actors and business men. Morgan

Johnson is home, stricken with a relapse at the news of the robbery of his bank; Doctor Peter Humphries was returned during the night—a hopeless leper. And nobody can understand how he could have developed such an advanced stage of leprosy in a few months. It takes years to develop scabs like his. Douglas Fenner, Anne Hale's producer, suddenly goes silent on us, and won't talk two cents' worth. The Right Honorable Albert Flood is murdered, and we can't even locate the logical suspect in the case—Nita van Sloan—"

McCrorty interrupted. "Do ye think it likely, Commissioner, that a bright young lady like Miss van Sloan would kill Flood and leave her gun and bag as evidence? And do you think, anyway, that a girl like her would commit murder?"

Kirkpatrick frowned. "I don't know what to think, Mac. But I'll tell you this—I want Nita van Sloan brought in. The evidence points to her, and it's our duty to place her under arrest and turn the case over to the District Attorney." He grimaced. "There's another one that's on our heels for action. He wants to get some convictions to show when election day comes around. All he needs is the evidence we've got, and he can convict Nita. I like the girl myself, but by God, if she's guilty of murder, I won't shield her!"

It was at this moment that the phone on Kirkpatrick's desk rang. He answered it, grunted once, then listened intently, his face flushing, and his fist clenching on the desk. At last he barked into the instrument: "All right, stay there. Keep tabs on him. Get a detail of half a dozen men to help you, and tail everybody that visits him!"

He hung up, and turned a sarcastic glance upon the assembled executives. "A fine police department we have here! It remained for a second grade detective to report in to his precinct house that Ben Laskar, the bookmaker, is in business again! That was the precinct captain just phoning. Laskar has an office in the Garmont Building, and he's making book again. *Not only that, gentlemen, but he's spreading the word in the Underworld that if anybody wants the Spider, all they have to do is contact Laskar.* He claims to be the Spider's contact man!"

McCrorty grinned. "That's pretty clever of the Spider. Laskar's a good man—even if he does make book. You going to pull him in for illegal betting, sir?"

"Not on your life!" Kirkpatrick grated. "I'm going to let Laskar lead me to the Spider! I begin to think, gentlemen, that the Spider's days are numbered!"

He sighed. "And now, let's map out a campaign for snaring this kidnap gang...."

CHAPTER 6
A CLUE IN THE AIR

A T NOON, while the conference was going on at police headquarters, Nita van Sloan was seated at a table in the dining room of the swanky Marion Hotel, where she had registered as Irene Rogers in accordance with Wentworth's instructions.

Wentworth had deliberately chosen the Marion as the place where she might best be safe from suspicion. Nita had donned a black wig, and had shaved her eyebrows to a thin, penciled line, then had dyed them coal black to match her hair. Olive tint cunningly applied to her face by Jackson, together with a pair of long jade earrings in her ears, had transformed her from a typical red-blooded, vivacious American girl, into a simpering Latin woman, at least five years older, with a look of worldly wisdom. Nita's native ability as an actress did the rest.

Here at the Marion, which was frequented by the *nouveau riche*, who delighted in paying the exorbitant room rentals that started at seven dollars per day, she was not likely to meet any of the people of her own set who might be likely to recognize her in spite of her disguise by some betrayal of mannerism.

A long, green, tight-fitting gown, bought by Jackson at her orders, had completed the change of personality, and Nita, looking at the finished work of disguise in her hotel room, had felt that not even Wentworth would recognize her. She had decided to tryout her artistry by boldly eating in the hotel dining room.

Now, as she sat over her *hors d'oeuvres*, she was applying herself mentally to the problem of the events of the morning. She had, of course, been aware of the kidnappings that had been going on for months. She knew also, that Wentworth was interesting himself in the case of Anne Hale, but she had not regarded it as a matter of major importance, and she was sure that Wentworth had likewise not suspected the deeply underlying criminal activity that lay behind the abduction of the beautiful actress.

But with the developments of the early morning, the case of Anne Hale assumed a deeply sinister significance. There was

NITA VAN SLOAN

every reason to believe that it was linked up with the disappearance and return of Morgan Johnson, and of Doctor Peter Humphries, as it must also be with the murder of the Right Honorable Albert Flood. The mystery of the apparently voluntary disappearance of Flood's sister, Lady Stella Flood, also needed to be explained. Could it be....

Suddenly, Nita's blood ran cold, and she felt an icy chill clutch at her heart. Idly, without thinking, she had been indulging in an old sport which she had learned from Wentworth, and which had come in handy on more than one occasion. That sport was the practice of lip-reading. In public places, where tables are placed far enough apart for privacy, people will converse with one another in absolute confidence that what they say will not be heard by anyone else. In fact, it is an old axiom among secret service men that a public place is the best spot to have confidential conversations, because there are no walls which may develop ears. Thus, the art of lipreading had often produced information not obtainable otherwise.

And now, as Nita ate and let her thoughts wander, she had been watching the two expensively dressed women at the table in the aisle next to hers. One of the women, a tall, dark, strikingly beautiful girl whose Russian sable coat was flung over her chair, was sitting with her back to Nita. The other woman, loud and flashily dressed, with her hands bedecked with diamonds, and a glittering cluster of stones in a pin at her breast, was facing the

girl with the Russian sable coat, and therefore facing Nita. It was that woman's lips which Nita had unconsciously been watching. THE WOMAN was speaking, keeping her voice very low; and without intending to do so, Nita followed what she was saying:

"I paid a visit to Morgan Johnson this morning," she was saying. "He's certainly out of his mind. I'm convinced that your doctor can do everything he says he can do."

The girl in the Russian sable made some reply which Nita could not get, and then the flashy woman continued. It was what she said now that shocked Nita into instant attention:

"I'm quite willing to pay forty thousand dollars, if your doctor can perform an operation to transplant into me the hormones from Anne Hale that will give me her acting ability. I've wanted all my life to be a great actress, and now that I have the money, I'm going to indulge myself. I've told my husband that I'm going out of town for two weeks. I have ten thousand dollars in cash, as you stipulated, and a check for the rest."

By a terrific application of will power, Nita forced herself to continue eating, while the terrible significance of the words she had just seen that woman's lips form filtered through her mind.

Could this possibly be a practical joke of some friends of hers? Yet she knew personally neither of these two women. And it would be a monstrous thing, even as a joke. Yet it would hardly be possible that such an operation could be performed; and it was even less believable that one woman should be willing to have a thing like that done to another woman in order to satisfy her vanity.

The flashy woman was speaking once more, her flabby face betraying a selfish, eager expression. "I'm ready to go with you now. This very minute... blindfolded in your car? Is that necessary? Oh, yes, I understand. Of course. I see. Very well, you may blindfold me when we enter your car...."

Almost sick at her stomach with nausea at the thought of what she had learned, Nita summoned a waiter and asked for her check. The waiter raised his eyebrows, remarking that madam had hardly begun her luncheon.

"Never mind," Nita said swiftly, affecting a Latin accent to blend with her appearance, "I've just remembered another appointment. My check, please!"

She laid down the money and the tip, rose quickly and passed into the lobby. At the desk where she inquired, there was not yet any message, either from Wentworth or from Mike Fogarty, who was to have reported to her here.

Moving quickly, with her eye on the dining room door, Nita seated herself at one of the desks, and wrote a note, informing Wentworth of what she had discovered. She took it back to the desk, said to the clerk: "If a gentleman should call on the telephone, please tell him there is a note for him. Do not read it to him, but ask him to call for it personally at once!"

"And the gentleman's name, madam?"

"It will not be necessary for him to give a name. Merely give him the note."

The clerk shrugged. "As you wish, madam."

Nita hurried from the hotel, walked down half a block, and flagged a taxi, got into it. "Wait here," she instructed the driver.

"I want to follow two women who will come out soon. You will be well paid."

While she waited, Nita checked over the small automatic pistol with which Jackson had supplied her, made sure that it was well oiled and in good working condition.

In a few moments the two women emerged from the hotel, and entered a long limousine that pulled in to the curb for them. Nita did not know it at the time, but the girl in the Russian sable coat was the same one whom Wentworth had already twice encountered in the early hours of the morning, once at the Citizens' Bank & Trust Company, and once at the home of Douglas Fenner, in Queens.

She could see from where she sat in the cab, that the older, flashily dressed woman was walking as if in a trance of eager expectation, her mouth twisted like a vampire's. And she was indeed a vampire, Nita reflected, who was going to do worse than drain the blood of a beautiful, talented young woman like Anne Hale. This business of transplanting hormones—Nita wondered if there was any truth in it.

Medical science had advanced by such great strides in the last few years that almost anything might be considered possible. Glands were shifted from monkeys to men, and from man to man. Was it not therefore, feasible, that a surgeon could transfer a person's talents to another person by means of transplanting hormones?

THE LIMOUSINE started away from the hotel, and Nita leaned forward, said to her driver: "Follow that car. You mustn't lose them. I'm afraid a girl's life depends on it. If you keep them in sight to their destination, I'll give you twenty dollars."

"Lady," said the cab driver, "for twenty dollars I'd murder them for you! Don't worry, we won't lose them."

They had not far to go. The limousine cut across to Fifth Avenue, then headed north past Fifty-seventh Street, then east to Third Avenue, then south again to Fifty-fourth Street. From there it swung west, up Madison, then west again, back to Fifth, and turned north.

Nita's driver remained about a hundred feet behind them, spurting ahead whenever he thought a red light might cut him off from them.

When they were back on Fifth Avenue, he said worriedly over his shoulder: "I'm afraid they're wise to us, lady, or else why would they double on their trail like that?"

"No, no," she told him. "They're doing it for another reason." She refrained from informing the cab driver that there was a blindfolded woman in that car, and that the twists and turns were being made so that she should not be able to guess in which direction they were finally going.

The limousine now drove straight up Fifth Avenue, and turned into a side street a few blocks below One Hundred and Tenth Street. It came to a halt before a row of four old brownstone houses that had apparently been renovated and converted into a single building by knocking down the inside walls. The whole front of the new building had been recently sandblasted, and the stoops removed, substituting a single entrance on the street level.

THE SPIDER

A small plaque alongside the entrance announced:

Doctor Kesten's
Private Sanatorium

The place looked respectable enough, except for one significant feature, which Nita noted as her cab drove slowly past the building—all the windows on the ground and upper floors were provided with steel shutters, and fully half of those shutters were closed.

The cab stopped at the far corner, and Nita looked back, saw that the girl in the Russian sable coat had gotten out, and was standing alongside the car, looking carefully up and down the street. Two or three pedestrians were passing, and across the street a number of school children were going home to lunch.

Apparently the girl in the sable coat was waiting for a favorable opportunity to conduct the blindfolded woman in the limousine across the sidewalk without attracting attention. Nita wondered how that could be done, and she thought that they had chosen a very bad hour of the day to bring their customer here. More and more children were coming around the corner from Fifth Avenue, and someone would surely notice the unusual phenomenon of a blindfolded woman being led across the sidewalk.

The cab driver got out from under his wheel, and came to stand beside the door. "Well, lady," he asked, "did I fill the bill?"

Nita nodded, not taking her eyes from the limousine. She extracted two ten-dollar bills from her purse, and handed them to him. She was wondering why a place like this had no back entrance, or some sort of driveway through which they could bring patients.

What she did not know was that there was a rear driveway, but that both the front and the rear of this sanatorium were being covered by two shadows placed there by Mike Fogarty, Wentworth's private detective. Fogarty was doing his job thoroughly, in his own plodding way. So far that morning he had located some twenty sanatoria in the city, anyone of which might or might not be the one Wentworth had in mind. And Fogarty had placed two men to watch each of them, one at the front and one at the rear.

He had been unsuccessful in picking up the man Toots, so he was compelled to resort to this method of checking on each possibility.

If Nita had thought of looking, she would have spotted Fogarty's operative, drinking cup after cup of coffee in the Coffee Pot diagonally across the street from Dr. Kesten's Sanatorium. But it did not occur to her that the place would be under surveillance.

The proprietor of the sanatorium had, however, thought of that possibility, and the operative in the front, as well as the one in the rear, had already been spotted. The plan which they were about to use for getting their client into the place without being observed was diabolical in its simplicity.

AS NITA watched from the taxicab, that plan clicked into operation. The first inkling that Nita had of it was when a series of staccato shots sounded at the corner, coming with the lightning speed and regularity which can be attained only by a machine gun. Someone down there was firing a machine gun, regardless of the school children returning home to lunch!

Nita's eyes were torn for an instant from the limousine. Looking down the long block of the side street, she could see the flashes of machine-gun fire coming from Central Park, across Fifth Avenue. She had a clear view of the corner, and she saw the policeman on traffic duty there clutch at his abdomen, and then topple forward, to lie still.

Her view of the policeman was blocked immediately by the crowds of panic-stricken children and other pedestrians who began to run in all directions in a frantic endeavor to escape the hail of lead that was spitting at them from the park.

What she failed to note was that Fogarty's operative came running out of the Coffee Pot, all thought of the sanatorium gone from his mind, yanking the gun from his shoulder holster and racing toward the scene of the shooting.

Fogarty's men were good men. They were brave. And it was that very bravery of the operative that spelled success for the plan. For now, a man leaned out from a first floor window of Dr. Kesten's Sanatorium, and signaled down to the girl in the sable coat.

At once the girl motioned to the chauffeur, who leaned in and helped the flashily dressed woman out to the sidewalk, hurrying her across to the entrance which was opened from within at once.

Nita did not miss that. Her breasts were heaving with excitement as she realized that the killing of the traffic policeman, the possible wounding or death of innocent women and children in the street, had all been perpetrated solely for the purpose of drawing attention away from the sanatorium for a moment or two.

No one in the street except Nita and her cab driver noticed the entrance of the flashily dressed woman. Instead of her hat, she was wearing a hood of some sort, with a white bandage tied across it; and Nita surmised that her ears had also been stopped up under the hood, so that she heard the shooting only vaguely, if at all. She would never be able to lead the police to the trail of Dr. Kesten's Sanatorium by giving them the clue that there had been a shooting in the vicinity.

Now, as Nita's small hands clenched with excitement, the door of the sanatorium closed, and the chauffeur leaped back into the limousine, and twisted around in his seat as if he had all this time been an interested spectator of the shooting scrape at the corner. The shooting had ceased as suddenly as it had begun. Men, women and children were milling around, still in frightened panic, and the car from which the spurts of machine gun fire had come was speeding northward up the north drive in Central Park.

A police car screamed up to the corner, and pedestrians pointed excitedly toward the park. There was no entrance into the park at this point, and the police patrol would have to drive up to One Hundred and Tenth Street to intercept the fleeing murder car. By that time, the machine gunners could easily desert their vehicle, and make their way out of the park, unmolested.

Nita's eyes burned with the intensity of her feeling as she

understood the diabolical cleverness of the plan. Only a man without heart or conscience could have conceived such a brutal, unnecessarily murderous method of diverting attention from his activity for a moment. It gave her an indication of the type of person at the head of the criminals they were fighting, but instead of instilling fear into her, it only quickened her resolve to smash the devil brain behind it all.

Ambulances were clanging up and down Fifth Avenue. With wet eyes, Nita saw several puny, pitiful bodies of school children being lifted into them by white-coated internes. The body of the policeman was being covered with a tarpaulin, pending the arrival of the medical examiner.

After a while, the Fogarty operative came back from the corner, and took up his station outside the Coffee Pot. The limousine eased into motion, pulled away. The operative was unaware that he had missed anything, unaware that the sudden, frightful death which had struck without warning at the corner had been perpetrated entirely for his benefit.

NITA TURNED to her cab driver, her face set with resolution. "I'm going into that sanatorium!" she announced.

The driver looked at her queerly. He was still shivering with the excitement of the shooting. "Gawd, lady, did you see all that? They got the cop cold! And them poor kids!"

He was so absorbed with his subject that he had not even heard what Nita said. The ambulances were departing, bearing their burdens of misery. Mothers, who had come running out of neighborhood houses at the news that their little ones were stricken down, were wailing in the street. The ambulances had come from two large nearby hospitals, but no medical aid had appeared from Dr. Kesten's Sanatorium. At first Nita thought that this was strange, since it might be expected that they would proffer aid to the wounded, being so near.

Of course, not being a registered hospital, they would not have ambulance service, and might argue that the two large hospitals in the vicinity could take care of the situation.

The police were beginning to go through the street, taking the names of witnesses. Nita had no desire to give her name to the police, so she ordered the cabby to drive away.

"Park somewhere near by," she told him. "We're coming back."

She estimated that the police should be through in about an hour, and she used the time to go into a restaurant and have a sandwich and a cup of coffee. She offered to buy the cabby lunch, and he accepted.

"What's your name?" she asked him.

He stuffed a spoonful of beef stew into his mouth, and answered: "Steve Miklos, lady."

"Look here, Steve, I want to get into that sanatorium."

He raised his eyes to hers. "Why don't you go in and ring the bell?"

"You don't understand. I want to get in there without their suspecting me. I think they're crooks."

"Haw! Begging your pardon, lady, I think you just got ideas from goin' to the movies. That dame wit' the muff on her head—I guess she was just one of the nuts that they take in. Don't you see, lady, it's a nut-house—a sanitarium!"

"No, no, it's not a sanitarium," she told him "It's a sanatorium.

A sanatorium is a place where they're supposed to treat sick patients, not where they confine insane people."

He scratched his head. "I never knew there was a difference, lady. But I still think you're imagining things. I suppose next, you'll be telling me that shooting at the corner had something to do with that sani-sanitarium!"

Nita sighed. There was no use trying to convince the driver. If she told him what she suspected that the whole shooting had been arranged just so as to get the woman into the place unobserved, he would think her insane. So she changed the subject.

"Listen," she said earnestly. "Never mind what that place is. Would you like to earn two hundred dollars by helping me to get into it?"

His eyes gleamed. "That's a lot of dough, lady. Would I have to take a chance on going to jail?"

"I don't think so." Slowly she spread out before him twenty ten-dollars bills from her purse. Luckily, Jackson had supplied her plentifully with money, and she was not loath to use it. "If you should be arrested, it wouldn't be more than a charge of reckless driving—and I'd guarantee not to press the case."

Miklos looked longingly at the money. "Just what do you want me to do, lady?"

"I'll tell you." Nita leaned over the table, whispered in his ear, explaining her plan.

At last Miklos nodded. "I'll do it, lady!"

"Good! Wait for me, while I make a phone call."

She went into the phone booth at the rear of the restaurant, and called the Hotel Marion, asked if there were any messages.

The room clerk told her: "That gentleman was just in, Miss Rogers, and I gave him your note. He read it, and seemed quite perturbed. He left word with me that if you called up I was to tell you to phone him at once at Mr. Fogarty's agency. He said you'd know the number."

Nita thanked him, hung up and called Mike Fogarty's office. Old Mike answered, himself. "Sure, Miss van Slo—I mean, Miss Rogers. Mr. Wentworth was just in. He was worried about your doin' something rash. Did you trail those two dames?"

"Yes. I've—found the place, Mr. Fogarty!"

"Ye don't say! Quick! Where is it?"

She gave him the address. "It's Dr. Kesten's Sanatorium. And I'm sure this is the right trail. These people are devils!"

She told him about the shooting on Fifth Avenue.

Fogarty said: "Hell, Miss Rogers, I've got two men covering that place. And those mugs just let the wool be pulled over their eyes! I wish I had you working for me!"

"Mr. Fogarty," Nita said resolutely, "I'm going in there."

"No, Miss Nita, you can't do that! Wentworth would skin me alive if I let you do that! He's gone up to interview Morgan Johnson, and he'll be back in a little while. You don't have to do anything like that—"

"I'm sorry, Mr. Fogarty, but my mind is made up. I'm going to find out who this Doctor Kesten really is—"

"But as long as you've got all this on them, we could go to the police and stage a raid—"

"And have our Doctor Kesten get away by some secret means of escape? You don't think that a man like that would leave himself without a last way out in case of a raid, do you? No, Mr. Fogarty, the only way is for someone to get in there and trap him. That someone is going to be I!"

She hung up before Fogarty could protest further.

CHAPTER 7
SURGEON'S SAMPLES

STEVE MIKLOS, the cab driver, was waiting for her at the table. She paid both checks, and they went out, drove to within a block of the sanatorium. Nita alighted from the cab, said to Miklos: "You know what to do?"

He nodded. "I got it straight, lady. Depend on me!"

Nita smiled bravely, turned and walked rapidly down the street, keeping on the opposite side from the sanatorium. The block had quieted down by this time, and except for a small knot of people near the corner, where men from Homicide were taking measurements of the street, there was little to indicate that death had visited here a short while ago.

When she was directly opposite the sanatorium, she glanced back, saw that Miklos' cab was coming in her direction. She waited a moment longer, till it was close, and she could hear the sound of the motor accelerating. Then she closed her eyes and stepped off the sidewalk, as if starting to cross the street directly in the path of the taxicab!

Miklos delayed putting on his brakes, and when he was practically upon her he swerved with the superb skill which only a New York taxicab driver possesses, and the cab slipped by Nita, with less than the width of a hair between the front fender and her body. The fender brushed her clothes, and Nita threw herself to one side, uttering a well simulated scream of anguish, which was almost drowned by the scream of Miklos' brakes.

Nita allowed herself to fall prone in the gutter, and she let her body grow limp, keeping her eyes closed.

In a moment a crowd had gathered around her, and someone was lifting her head. She had previously removed all rouge and lipstick from her face, and had powdered it generously, so that she looked as pale as death.

She could hear Miklos' voice raised in protestation as he acted out the part she had assigned to him. "Gee, she walked right into my car. I guess the fender must of struck her in the side. My Gawd, *this* is terrible!"

Nita felt herself lifted in strong arms.

A voice said: "Must be internal injuries. She needs first aid. Somebody ring in for an ambulance—"

Steve Miklos interrupted: "There's a sanatorium right here. Take her in. They must have a doctor—"

Nita lay limp while she was carried across the street. Someone opened the door, and she was carried into an elevator, then into a room that smelled strongly of chloroform. She did not open her eyes as she was placed in a soft bed.

Professional fingers began to remove her clothing, and she heard a woman's voice say: "I can't see any bruises, Doc. She must have suffered internal injuries."

They had taken off all her clothing, and thrown a sheet over her. While she was being carried into the building, Nita had held her small twenty-two calibre pistol in the palm of her hand, and as she was placed upon the bed she had fallen forward on her face, taking the opportunity to slip the weapon under the pillow with a quick motion.

Now she felt the professional fingers of a physician probing her body. Those fingers sent cold shudders up and down her spine. Somehow they seemed to have been dipped in some alchemist's jug of evil. She forced herself to remain limp until the examination was over.

The physician's voice drummed at her ears, and she was suddenly sure that she was hearing Doctor Kesten speak: "I don't see anything the matter with her, Miss Flood. Perhaps she has fainted from shock."

The man sounded cultured, educated. But there was a flat coldness about his voice, an impersonal cruelty that was almost unbelievable.

Nita risked opening one eye a hair's breadth. She *had* to get a look at this man, had to see his face.

HER DISAPPOINTMENT was acute. The doctor was gowned in a long, surgical robe, and he wore a white cap and antiseptic mask, larger than that usually used in hospitals, so that the only visible portions of his face were his eyes and a short strip of forehead.

Nita stole another glance around the room at the nurse, and she barely restrained a start of surprise. The nurse, attired all in white now, was the girl in the Russian sable coat whom she had followed from the Marion Hotel.

"Doc" went on speaking: "It is rather inconvenient, having

Nita followed Kesten into the office. She did not hear the corridor door swing open.

this woman brought in just at this time. We can't afford to have her conscious, and intruding in our business. Give her an opiate, Miss Flood. Keep feeding it to her so that she remains unconscious for the rest of the day—"

The nurse had been standing facing "Doc," both hands pressed against her breasts, her face flushed. Now she broke in abruptly, speaking swiftly as if the floodgates of emotion had suddenly burst.

"You—you devil!" she screamed. "You fiend! I won't help you any longer. I won't be a party to your hellish schemes. You made me help in the bank robbery because of my brother. You made me drive out to Fenner's home for the same reason. You promised no one would be killed, And now, when I brought that woman here today, I expected you would use some clever ruse to evade the shadowers. Instead you staged a wholesale murder. Little children—" She covered her face with both hands. "I can still see their pitiful bodies, twisted in pain, with bullets in their stomachs!"

She tore her hands from her face, advanced upon Kesten, beating with her fists against his chest. "You told me it was just a confidence game—that no one would ever be hurt or killed. And now I see people dying, mutilated, all through you—and with my help. I tell you I'm through! Through! Through—"

Her voice rose in a shrill scream that sounded throughout the building. "I'm going to get the Spider! I'm going to tell him everything!"

She started for the door, and Doctor Kesten snarled, struck at her with his clenched fist. The blow staggered the girl, and she almost dropped to one knee, but recovered, and leaped for the door again. Kesten ripped out an oath, reached forth a hand and twined it in her hair, dragged her back. The girl gasped with the pain of it, struggling feebly against the punishing grip.

"No, my dear, you won't talk any more. You won't tell the Spider a thing—because dead women can't talk!"

His hand reached to a cabinet, where row upon row of gleaming scalpels lay.

And Nita van Sloan sat up suddenly in the bed, her hand reaching under the pillow and coming out with the pistol. She leveled it at the man, and called out in a steady, cold voice:

"Let her go, Doctor Kesten!"

The man stiffened. Still gripping the girl's hair, he twisted around, looked into the vicious little barrel of Nita's automatic. Nita did not repeat her command.

Slowly, Kesten released his grip on the girl's hair.

Kesten turned to face the bed. "So you were playing 'possum!'" he snarled. "You—"

Suddenly he broke off, whirled to the door. But he was too late. Miss Flood had yanked it open, and dashed out, running with desperate urgency.

Kesten cursed, started after her, but Nita called out: "I'm shooting!"

Kesten stopped short, and turned around. His eyes lanced hatred at Nita, but he stood still. The quality of her voice told him that she would not be afraid to shoot.

"Close the door!" Nita ordered crisply.

He obeyed. "Who are you?" he demanded.

She didn't bother to answer. "Now turn around while I get some clothes on."

Reluctantly he turned around under the persuasion of the pistol. Nita reached out and picked up a nightgown which lay on the bed. Still keeping Kesten covered, she managed to slide into it, then stood up. Out of the corner of her eye she saw a door in the side wall.

"You can turn around," she told him. "Put your hands up, and walk slowly into the next room."

He said nothing, but the small eyes above the surgical mask glowed with an unholy light. Nita followed Kesten into the office. As she stepped through the connecting door, she did not see the corridor door of her own room swing open, did not see the twisted face of the man in the attendant's costume who peered in. Had she seen him, she might not have recognized him. But Wentworth would have known the man; so would Fogarty; so would a good number of detectives on the New York Police Force.

The man was Nick Tootsler, known in the Underworld as Toots.

HIS FACE was long and sharp, and did not follow a straight line, so that although the bridge of his nose was between his eyes, the tip of his nose fell almost directly under his left eye. His mouth was also twisted, giving the effect to his long face of a sort of attenuated gargoyle.

Nita did not see him, but pushed into the office after Kesten. The doctor stood facing her, with his hands raised, but carefully watching for an opportunity to spring at her.

He spoke in his coldly impersonal voice. "Whoever you are, you've put yourself in a tight spot, young woman. You won't leave this place alive. You must know something about us, or you wouldn't have tricked us into admitting you this way. Well, you'll never know any more—"

Nita cut in coldly. "I'm going to know more, right now. I'm going to know who you are. *Dr. Kesten, take off that mask!*"

"And if I refuse?"

"I'll shoot you between the eyes."

"You're a woman. You wouldn't dare. You wouldn't kill a man in cold blood—"

"You're not a man. You're a fiend. I know some of the things you're doing here. You made Morgan Johnson an idiot, and you forced him to help rob his own bank. You turned Dr. Peter Humphries into a leper. You're going to perform some unspeakable operation on poor Anne Hale—"

"Tut, tut, my dear. You shouldn't believe all these stories you hear. This place is always open to inspection. If you think all those things are true, why didn't you bring the police—"

"Because I knew you'd have some means of covering up, or of escaping. Now, Doctor Kesten, I'm through talking. Take off that mask."

Kesten smiled, and said: *"All right, Toots!"*

And Toots, who had stolen up behind Nita, brought a blackjack down with vicious force on the back of her head.

The breath escaped from Nita's lungs with a *whoosh*. She wilted, and the pistol dropped from her nerveless fingers. She collapsed on the floor, like an empty sack.

Kesten watched gravely while Toots picked her up and carried her back to the bed, dropped her on it roughly, then returned to the office.

"She won't wake up for a while, Doc!"

Kesten's voice was sharp. "Where were you, you fool! The Flood girl just escaped!"

Toots gasped. "Escaped? What do mean? I seen her going out the front door, but I didn't think nothin' of it. She goes an' comes all the time—"

"Well, this time she's gone for good. She's through. She's going to squeal!"

Toots twirled his blackjack, his face becoming even more twisted than before. "Well, what do you know about that! I thought she would stay on account of her brother."

"It got to be too much for her. I didn't judge her correctly."

"If she's goin' to the cops wit' her story, we got nothin' to worry about, boss. In case of a raid they couldn't find a thing—"

"It's not the cops I'm worried about, Toots. She said she's going to the Spider. That's the one man I fear. He's an intelligent antagonist." Kesten shrugged. "Well, we'll worry about that when the time comes."

"Say, boss!" Toots suddenly exclaimed. "Did she say she was going to see the Spider!"

"That's what she said. But I can't imagine how she expects to get in touch with him—"

"I'll tell you, boss! She must of heard me talking to a couple of the boys, downstairs. We was talkin' about Ben Laskar, the guy that got away from us at the bank job. He's set himself up in business—makin' book. An' he's also spread the word around that anybody what wants the Spider should contact Laskar. He's the Spider's go-between!"

Kesten's eyes glittered. "That explains a lot, Toots. It explains what happened at the bank job. Tell you what you do, Toots. Take two of the boys and go to this office of Laskar's. See if you can head off the Flood girl. *And try to make Laskar tell you where to find the Spider!*"

Toots grinned. "Okay, boss. I'm on the way!"

WHEN THE gunman had gone, Doctor Kesten stood for a long time in silent thought. Then he pressed a button, and in a moment an attendant answered his signal. This man was also hard-faced, like Toots, and there was the visible bulge of a shoulder holster under his white jacket.

"Kyle!" the Doctor ordered. "There's a girl in the next room. She's unconscious. Take her down into the sub-cellar. Prepare the mixing machine. We'll put her in tonight."

Kyle grinned. "Right, boss. I like to hear 'em yell when the gears starts meshin' on 'em!"

Kyle went into the next room, and Kesten rubbed his hands as if he had just disposed of a vexing problem. Then he went out through the corridor door, went down a flight of stairs, and walked to the rear of the building. Here, he pressed the palm of his hand against a spot in the wall, and a door slid open, revealing a staircase down into a passageway. He followed this passage for about fifty yards, then mounted another rickety flight of stairs, pressed his hand against the wall once more, and stepped through the sliding door, which closed at once behind him. He was in a sort of closet. He opened the door of this closet, and entered an office similar to the one in the building he had just left.

The flashy looking woman was sitting here, waiting with impatience. The shutters of this room were closed on the outside, so the woman couldn't see the street.

This office was in another brownstone building, fifty yards down the street from the sanatorium; and it was the reason why Kesten did not fear a raid. For this was the place where he conducted his criminal activities, while the sanatorium itself was only a blind.

The flashy woman rose as he entered, and exclaimed: "You were away so long, doctor—"

"Something entirely unavoidable, madam, I assure you. Now, shall we get down to business?"

"Yes, yes, sure. See, I've brought the cash for you. It's in thousand-dollar bills. You can count it if you like—"

He took the money, dropped it negligently on the desk. "That is the down payment. Now, as to the balance—"

She wagged a finger at him. "After the operation, doctor, after the operation. When it's over, I'll give you my check for thirty thousand dollars." Her face was flushed with gross excitement, which overlay the basic coarseness that was written there. She was the widow of a man who had become extremely wealthy through a series of fraudulent stock transactions, and who had then died. Now she was out to get as much as she could out of life, and she didn't care who suffered in the process. "You transplant those hormones for me, doctor, so I get Anne Hale's ability, and I'll pay you."

Kesten smiled. "My dear Mrs. Fleshmore! You must realize that the price I am charging for the operation is very low—considering the—er—risks I take. The check will have to be made out in advance."

She hesitated. "How do I know that you have Anne Hale here?"

"Come!" was all he said.

He led the way out of the office, into a short hall, which ended at a solid oak door. At the right of this hall was the open door of an operating room, but the oak door at the end of the hall was shut tight.

Kesten fitted a key into it, swung it open. The sight that met the eyes of Mrs. Fleshmore caused her to gasp.

THERE WAS a long room, divided by a corridor in the middle. On either side of the corridor was a row of glass cages, each containing a human being. There were men and women, all chained to the wall so that their hands were high above their heads. All of them were nude, and they were all blindfolded.

"These," Kesten said with a touch of pride, "are some of my samples!" He pointed to one of the cages, the third from the end, on the right. "There, Mrs. Fleshmore, is Anne Hale! For forty thousand dollars, I will transfer her ability to you!"

The glistening white body of the great actress, Anne Hale, hung, suspended by her hands. At intervals her body writhed and twisted with the torture of her position, but there was no relief. She was semi-conscious.

"If you would prefer to become a great artist," Kesten went on, "I could give you the ability of the inimitable Stromboni, in the second cage here. The others, I regret to say, are all sold, and the operations contracted for."

Mrs. Fleshmore's first glance had shocked her. Now the sadistic nature of her mean soul came to the fore, and her small eyes glittered with pleasure at sight of the suffering of these kidnapped people. Her gaze travelled avidly up and down the rows of cages, containing naked men and women whose genius was something she envied. She gloried in their suffering.

"Do you keep them like this all the time?" she asked.

"Oh, no. I put them up for an hour or so a day, just to keep them tame. If any of them should become recalcitrant, they know they will be left to bang by the arms for a longer period. It's amazing how docile they become when I threaten to hang them by the arms for a whole day. The agony, you understand, is absolutely unbearable if it is stretched beyond an hour."

Mrs. Fleshmore breathed a deep sigh of contentment. "I'll pay you—in advance, Dr. Kesten!"

He bowed politely, closed the door of the unspeakable exhibit, and led her back to the office. She sat down at the desk, wrote out a check for forty thousand dollars. "To whom shall I make this payable?" she asked.

"To cash, dear lady," the doctor told her.

She signed the check, handed it over. "I've O.K.'d it for cash, as you see, so you can send a Western Union Messenger for the money if you wish."

"Thank you, madam." Kesten pressed a button, and an attendant appeared.

Kesten's manner suddenly changed. "Take this woman down to the mixing machine!" he ordered. "Get her ready. We'll put her in tonight."

Mrs. Fleshmore stared at him blankly. "Mixing machine?" she asked puzzledly.

Kesten smiled thinly. "You are not going to be operated on in the way you think, Mrs. Fleshmore," he explained. "Your check is going to be cashed, and then, tonight, you will be ground up in a mixing machine in our cellar. What is left of you will then be soaked in lye for forty-eight hours—and presto! There will be nothing at all left!"

"You—you mean you're going to kill me?"

"You are very bright. Some of our clients don't get the idea for quite a while!"

"B-but what about the operation?"

"There will be no operation. Such an operation is an utter impossibility. Only the vicious and gullible believe it to be possible. I have sold the Anne Hale operation five times already, and I am making another sale tonight. The lady who is buying the operation tonight is just a little less gullible than you, my dear Mrs. Fleshmore. She insists that she actually see me start to operate on Anne Hale before she pays. But—" Kesten's eyes twinkled with an evil light—"I'm quite sure Miss Hale won't object to a little cutting—if I promise not to hang her up by the arms tomorrow!"

Mrs. Fleshmore was slumped in her chair, pallid faced, her

eyes closed. While Kesten talked, she had understood the evil in the man's mind, had seen how her own cruelty and ruthlessness had led her to her doom. And she read in his voice the utter finality of her fate. She would never leave this place alive. The realization had struck at her consciousness, and she slumped in a dead faint.

Kesten motioned toward her contemptuously, said to the attendant: "Take her away. I'll be back in an hour or so. I'm going out to cash this check!"

CHAPTER 8
THE CONTACT MAN

T HE OFFICE which Ben Laskar had established was on Broadway, in the heart of the Times Square district. Prodigious work had been done on it since the night before. Certain alterations had been made, which connected the adjoining office to Laskar's through a filing closet which had been installed. A dictograph enabled anyone in the adjoining office to overhear and record any conversation which took place here.

There was no name on the door of the adjoining office, but Laskar's door bore gilt letters on the plate glass, with his name.

Now, he sat at his desk, facing Miss Flood, the girl who had escaped from Dr. Kesten's Sanatorium with the aid of Nita. The girl was talking rapidly, and Laskar was listening.

"I've got to see the Spider! They say that you're the Spider's contact man. Please, take me to him!"

Laskar studied her carefully. "I'm not admitting anything,

Miss. But for the sake of the argument, supposing I could put you in touch with the Spider, what's your reason for wanting to see him?"

"I'm Stella Flood—Lady Stella Flood, they call me in England."

Laskar whistled. "The sister of Albert Flood, who was murdered yesterday?"

Stella Flood paled. "Oh, God! They killed him anyway! And Kesten promised he wouldn't! Kesten promised if I'd help him he'd let my brother go!"

She slumped into a chair, and quietly began to weep.

Laskar tried to soothe her. "Suppose you begin at the beginning, Miss."

She raised wet eyes. "Yes, yes. I'll tell you everything—if you'll let me see the Spider!"

"Telling me is the same as telling the Spider, Miss," Laskar informed her. "Go ahead."

"M-my brother, Albert, was kidnapped the day after we landed in this country. He's been kept prisoner all this time, by Doctor Kesten."

"But that's impossible, Miss. Albert Flood gave a reception last night—"

"You don't understand. That wasn't Albert. That was one of Kesten's own men."

"His own man? But the man looked just like your brother—"

"Of course. I forgot I didn't tell you about Kesten. That isn't his real name. He's never shown his face. But whoever he is, he has great talent in those fingers of his. He's a great facial surgeon.

111

"Did you want me?" the Spider asked in a gentle voice.

All those people he's kidnapped, and that were supposed to have returned—well, Kesten still has them prisoners. But he operated on other men, modeled their faces after those of his prisoners, and sent them back. Morgan Johnson is still his prisoner. The man who made Stryker open the front door of the bank was really Kesten's man, upon whom Kesten had operated. And Peter Humphries—Kesten always told me that was his masterpiece, but I don't know why. He took a leper and operated on the man's face so that he resembled Humphries. And no one could understand how Humphries could have developed such advanced stages of leprosy in such a short time."

Laskar was staring at her almost unbelievingly. "You're sure of all this, Miss?"

"Sure? Of course I am. God help me, I've acted as Kesten's assistant in his villainies. I inveigled old dowagers who wanted operations to acquire the abilities and looks of younger persons. At first, Kesten told me it was a confidence game, that he wanted to get their money, and then there would be no operation. He made me help by giving me the hope that my brother would be released. And now, I'm not fit to live any longer—"

"That's right, sister," a harsh voice abruptly broke in on her, "you ain't gonna live any longer!"

SHE SWUNG around, gasping, to face Toots and two other men who had stepped into the office with drawn guns. Two of the men seized her by the arms, while Toots covered Laskar.

"Sit where you are!" Toots snarled.

Stella Flood shrieked: "Damn you, Toots, you killed my brother!"

113

Toots grinned twistedly. "Yeah, sister. Our man went for a walk, an' we met him wit' your brother. Our man had picked up this here Van Sloan dame's bag in the house, so we used her gun to bump your brother. So what?"

Stella Flood struggled to get out of the grip of the two gunmen, trying to get at him. But she was held in a firm, cruel grip, and her struggles were useless.

Toots sneered at her, and walked around the desk, standing behind Laskar. "Listen, bo," he said, disregarding Stella Flood, "I wanna get a little information outta you. You gonna give it easy, or you gonna give it hard?"

Laskar gripped the arms of his chair, and looked up fearlessly at the other.

"Hard," he said.

Toots grinned sadistically. "That's okay by me!"

He whipped out a large bandana handkerchief, twisted it into a rope, and whipped it around Laskar's throat from behind. Then he twisted the barrel of his gun into the knot, using it as a tourniquet. The twisted handkerchief contracted about Laskar's throat, and the veins stood out on his forehead from the sudden agony.

Toots grinned, and twisted a little harder. "All I wanna know, bo, is where we can put the finger on the Spider. When you're ready to talk, raise your hand!"

Laskar stubbornly refused to yield, and the bandanna tightened inexorably about his throat.

Stella Flood shrieked, and one of the men struck her in the face.

Toots demanded: "Well, where's the Spider?"

And suddenly, as if it had been arranged like a stage entrance, the long double doors of the filing closet were flung open, and the three men stared in stupefaction at the tall, cloaked figure of the Spider, standing there with empty hands folded across his chest.

"Did you want me?" the Spider asked in gentle voice.

Three guns were instantly trained upon the Spider. Involuntarily, Toots released his pressure upon the bandanna, and Laskar gasped: "I thought you were never coming Spider!"

"I'm sorry, Ben, I was delayed. I see these rats almost had you down!"

"I'll say!" Laskar exclaimed, rubbing his throat. Toots had covered the Spider with a second gun, in his left hand. Now he sneered. "So you're the Spider! Well, how's it feel for three guys to have the drop on you? Say your prayers, guy. The boss has promised us a bonus for your hide!"

"I don't think I'll accommodate you, Toots. The only reason I allowed the proceedings to go so far is that I wanted your confession to murder, Toots. Your story of how you killed Albert Flood is duly recorded on a dictograph record in the next office. When I kill you, the police will not be able to blame me."

"Kill me!" Toots laughed his derision. "Why—"

"I'm going to kill you now!"

Almost in accompaniment to those words, the Spider's hands flashed in and out from shoulder holsters with such blinding speed that neither Toots nor his two men knew what was happening until twin blazing streaks of flame poured from the Spider's two automatics. Men had often told of the amazing, hardly believable skill of the Spider with his guns. But those tales were largely discounted, because there was no living witness to the stories. Those who faced the Spider's guns never survived to tell the tale.

Now, three shots flared from his guns—two from the left hand one, a single shot only from the right hand one. Each shot sped true to its mark, as if the name of its victim had been engraved upon it.

The two thugs holding Stella Flood were hurled backward before they could pull their triggers, and they crashed against the wall, slumped down, dead before they hit the floor, each with a bullet between the eyes.

Stella Flood rushed forward, and it was her misfortune that she moved just at the moment when Toots fired his only shot. That shot was fired by the reflex action of the hand of a man already dead, for the Spider's shot had caught him between the eyes, just like the other two. Toots had dashed for the window at the same time that he fired, and when he was hit his heavy body crashed through the pane of glass, slumping half in and half out.

But that shot that he had fired had already done its damage. It struck Stella Flood squarely through the heart.

As the last reverberations of the heavy gunfire died away, the Spider stepped into the room, moved from one to another of the dead men. On the forehead of each he left his trademark—the crimson impression of a spider. Then he went and stood over the body of Stella.

"It's better this way," he said to Laskar. "She had to die. To live on, with the picture of the things she helped to do for her brother's sake, would have been torture!"

Laskar was still rubbing his neck, but he was paying no attention to the dead Stella Flood. "God!" he exclaimed. "I never saw such shooting! No wonder they're afraid of you!"

There were the sounds of commotion from out in the hallway, and the Spider stepped quickly back into the closet. "I'm leaving, Ben. Show the police the dictograph records in the next room. Toots' confession will serve to clear a certain young lady who is under suspicion for the murder of Stella's brother. When the place is cleaned up again, start business once more. You'll hear from me."

"W-where are you going?" Laskar demanded.

"I'm going," the Spider said grimly, "to clean up the rest of this gang!"

And he disappeared into the closet just as the corridor door opened to a bluecoat....

CHAPTER 9
THE CURTAIN RISES
ON DEATH

DOWNSTAIRS ON Broadway, in front of the building where Laskar's office was located, a radio police car was already parked at the curb, and a squad car from the precinct house was pulling in with squealing brakes. A uniformed sergeant and a detective from the squad car were forcing back all those who attempted to leave the building.

"Everybody back!" the sergeant shouted. "Nobody leaves till we've checked on them! What's the trouble? Murder—that's what!"

Frightened men and women pressed back into the lobby, while the bluecoats from the radio car set up a cordon in front of the building. The plainclothes man left the sergeant on guard, ran to the elevator bank, and demanded of the starter: "Where was the shooting? Who phoned in?"

"I-I'll take you up," the starter stammered. "There's a policeman up there already. It's in Ben Laskar's new office. S-somebody said it was the Spider did the shooting!"

While the detective went up with the starter, and while the uniformed sergeant conscientiously prevented all people from leaving the building, Richard Wentworth, minus his Spider cloak and hat, sauntered carelessly out through a side street entrance of the adjoining building. His own foresight, and Jackson's efficiency in arranging for the office space for Laskar, had made this escape possible.

The adjoining building was separated from Laskar's building only by a narrow areaway, and Wentworth had merely stepped from one fire escape to another, carrying his hat and cloak rolled under his arm. These he had deposited in the additional office which Jackson had rented for him in the side street building, without the knowledge of Ben Laskar.

Thus, he was able to step out to freedom, while the police smugly thought that they had the Spider bottled up.

Wentworth strolled around the corner to Broadway, and joined the throng of curiosity seekers who had gathered at the first sign of trouble. He watched with interest while the various members of the homicide squad arrived, followed shortly thereafter by Commissioner Kirkpatrick in person.

Wentworth's eyes bore a serious expression. He was quite sure that Kirkpatrick was a reasonable man; and once the Commissioner had heard the dictograph recording of Stella Flood's statements, together with Tootsler's confession, Kirkpatrick would without doubt order an immediate raid on the Kesten Sanatorium. Wentworth meant to be on hand when that raid took place; he was grimly resolved that no harm should come to Nita van Sloan.

In the person of Richard Wentworth, friend of the Commissioner, he could pass through the cordon of police, join the Commissioner in Laskar's office, and suggest the raid.

He was about to do this—had, in fact, started to push through the crowd, when he suddenly noticed a taxicab that was slowly cruising down Broadway, close to the curb. It was not the cab itself that attracted his attention, but the white face of its passenger, pressed close to the window.

He knew her in an instant.

It was Anne Hale, the actress, who had been kidnapped— the girl on whose behalf Douglas Fenner had appealed for the Spider's help!

Impulsively, Wentworth swung toward that cab. And he checked the impulse on the instant.

For his keen eye had caught sight of the second cab, trailing close behind the first. He stood stock still, affecting not to notice either of the vehicles, while they passed. But out of the corner of

The attack had come! Wentworth fired
without even crossing his hands.

his eye he studied the faces of the two narrow-eyed thugs who were seated, leaning forward, in the pursuing taxi. The men were wearing overcoats, but Wentworth could see the white jackets under those overcoats, and he saw the white uniform caps that they wore.

Those two men were attendants from a hospital or sanatorium. And they were trailing Anne Hale!

THE ACTRESS'S cab moved slowly down the street, and pulled up in the next block. The two thugs alighted from their cab, and walked swiftly forward, their hands significantly in their pockets.

One of them pulled open the door and stepped quickly inside, while the other climbed in alongside the driver.

Wentworth's trained mind grasped the situation at once. Anne Hale must have managed in some way to escape from her captors, and they had followed her. No doubt they had instructions to bring her back at all costs. What puzzled him was the question of why she was here. A girl who had just escaped from such horrors as Anne Hale must have experienced would surely have gone to the police; instead, here she was, riding down Broadway in a taxicab.

But Wentworth wasted no time on conjecture. Those thoughts skimmed through his mind even as he swung into action. He had already covered the distance between himself and the cab.

He could see that the thug in the front seat was pressing some object into the driver's side, and the driver was beginning to pull the car away from the curb.

Wentworth's hand slid in and out from his shoulder holster, appearing with one of his automatics, even as he leaped to the running board, wrenched open the door and swung himself inside.

He caught one single glimpse of Anne Hale's frightened face, of the girl crouching back into the cushions of the seat, while the thug beside her menaced her with a gun. Then the thug turned, startled, and snarled at sight of the intruder, twisted around to bring his gun to bear upon Wentworth.

Wentworth grinned thinly, and slashed down hard with the barrel of his automatic, catching the thug in the right temple. Flesh and skin scraped, and blood appeared. The man cried out, tried to raise his gun, but Wentworth smashed him hard in the mouth with a short left jab, then knotted his right fist about the automatic and crashed a terrific right to the man's chin. The thug emitted a long, hissing sigh, and curled up in the seat, limp against the shuddering, wide-eyed Anne Hale.

Wentworth twisted around and slipped into the seat along-side the unconscious thug, and faced forward. The thug in the front seat had turned around, and was gasping in amazement. He withdrew his gun from the driver's side, and started to raise it, but froze into immobility as he found himself staring into the muzzle of Wentworth's automatic.

Wentworth said tightly: "Push down the safety catch on that gun, and let it drop!"

The thug's face was twisted into a mask of hate and fear. But he obeyed. He started to raise his hands above his head, but Wentworth snapped: "Keep them down. Don't try to attract attention!"

The driver slowed down the cab, pulling in to the curb. Wentworth kept the thug covered, and called to the cabby: "Keep going, friend. You won't be harmed, and I'll pay you well." He gave the address of the Hopecrest Apartments on Central Park West. "Drive there, and I'll pay you off—"

"But how about the police, mister?" the cabby demanded. "I'll get in Dutch. They'll take away my license—"

"They won't bother you. Here, take a look at this!"

Still keeping the thug covered, Wentworth extracted from his pocket the special card which had long ago been given him by Commissioner Kirkpatrick. It stated that Richard Wentworth Esq., was "hereby appointed an honorary Deputy Commissioner of the Police Department of the City of New York...."

That card had been issued by Kirkpatrick many months ago, in a moment of extreme thankfulness, at a time when Wentworth had rendered an extraordinary service. Kirkpatrick had forgotten about that card, or he would have revoked it. Now, it came in handy. The driver was not convinced, but he was impressed. And with the temptation of the hundred dollars which Wentworth thrust at him, he permitted himself to be swayed.

"Okay, Mister Wentworth. But you gotta take care of me!" He swung around the block, and headed north toward the Hopecrest Apartments.

ANNE HALE remained silent, looking at Wentworth with a sort of startled admiration. She was a very beautiful girl, and it was easy to understand why she had been acclaimed by New Yorkers as the premiere dramatic actress of her day. She was wearing a cloth coat with a fur collar, and Wentworth gasped as she allowed the coat to fall open; for she wore not a bit of clothing, under that coat!

She caught his glance, flushed prettily, and pulled the coat close about her. "W-where are you taking me, Mister Went-worth?" she asked.

"To my home," he told her. "Apparently you don't want the police, or you'd have gone to them already."

She seemed to take for granted his presence here, and his readiness to help her. "That's true. Let me explain—"

"Wait. We'll be home soon, and you can tell me all about it." He added grimly: "There are a number of things I'll want to know!"

Under Wentworth's direction, the cab driver drove around the block, behind the Hopecrest Apartments, and in through the alley alongside the church. Garage number one was unoc-cupied, and the cab entered as the electric eye automatically opened the back door. In a few moments Ram Singh, who had returned from the country, came down with Jackson, and aided in bringing up the two thugs. The one whom Wentworth had knocked out was still unconscious, and Ram Singh carried him. The other was glad to obey Jackson's order to march.

Wentworth paid off the cab driver, and watched him pull out of the garage. "Remember," he told the man, "if the police should come here now, I'll know you sent them. I've got your number and your name. I know where to find you."

"Don't worry, Mister Wentworth," the driver called back. "I know how to keep my mouth shut. You're a guy I'd rather have for a friend than an enemy!"

Wentworth shut the garage door, and conducted Anne Hale through the basement to his private elevator, and up into the penthouse apartment. Jackson brought her a sandwich and a drink of smooth cognac that brought color to her cheeks.

Wentworth watched her eat, then when she sat back, he said to her soberly: "Now, Miss Hale, suppose you tell me everything that happened to you since you were kidnapped."

She began to talk quickly, as if she wanted to get the things she had to tell off her mind.

"The men who kidnapped me blindfolded and drugged me. When I awoke, I was in a cage in a room with a dozen other cages. I was hanging by the wrists, and the blindfold was still on my eyes. I knew there were other cages in the room, because every once in a while I heard the hateful voice of that Doctor Kesten, explaining things to some visitor. He would bring gullible people with money to this room, and offer to operate on one of us prisoners, to give his client our peculiar abilities. They believed him."

Wentworth nodded slowly. "He must be a good salesman—"

"He's worse! He's a devil! He hung us by our wrists for hours every day, just to tame us, as he said."

She paused for a moment, looked at him queerly. "You think it strange that I accept you without question, Mr. Wentworth? Don't you think it strange that I trust you like this, confide in you?"

He studied her. "There is a reason?"

"Yes," she nodded quickly. "I've heard a good deal about you— from Nita van Sloan!"

Wentworth leaned forward in his chair. "From Nita—"

"She's a prisoner in that devil's workshop, Mr. Wentworth.

We were together for a few minutes, and she told me about herself and about you. Mr. Wentworth, you must save her quickly. Kesten is going to operate on her—"

"Operate? I thought that was just a sham. Why—"

"He's going to operate, some time in the early hours of the morning. It's not to delude some gullible victim this time, Mr. Wentworth, but out of sheer deviltry. He knows who she is, knows that she is allied to some enemy of his known as the Spider—and he says he's going to send her back to the Spider, with her body and face so horribly disfigured and twisted that no one will even be able to look at her. He's—he's going to cut off her nose, and—and her breasts—"

Wentworth's eyes grew bleak and cold, and Anne Hale broke off, uttering a slight gasp at what she saw in them. He had planned to be present when Kirkpatrick heard the dictograph recordings. He had planned to make sure that Kirkpatrick took him along on the raid which he was sure to make. But now he had allowed himself to be sidetracked by this incident, and he would not be able to assist in the rescue of Nita.

If Kesten knew that Nita was connected with the Spider, he would make sure to carry out in some measure his plans for revenge, if the raid took place.

SWIFTLY WENTWORTH picked up the telephone, dialed the private number of Ben Laskar's office.

As he expected, a patrolman answered the call.

"This is Richard Wentworth," he told the officer. "I want to talk to Commissioner Kirkpatrick."

"Sorry, sir," he was told, "the Commissioner has left."

Wentworth raced the horse
from the deadly cross-fire.

"Where's he gone?" Wentworth demanded tensely.

"We-ell," the bluecoat answered cautiously, "I ain't supposed to say—"

"It's perfectly all right. You know I'm a friend of the Commissioner's. Tell me—has he gone on a raid?"

"We-ell, yes—"

Abruptly, Wentworth hung up. He clicked the receiver, got Jackson at the switchboard downstairs. "Get me Kesten's Sanatorium on the phone!" he ordered.

In a moment he was connected. He sighed as he heard the

welcome voice of Commissioner Stanley Kirkpatrick at the other end.

"Kirk!" he exclaimed. "Then you did make the raid!"

"Yes, Dick. How did you know—"

"Never mind! Did you find Nita? Is she safe?"

"Hell, Dick, we haven't found a thing. We've been through this place with a fine tooth comb. It's as clean as a whistle. There's no sign of Anne Hale, or of any of the other prisoners that those dictograph records spoke of. Kesten isn't here. We've questioned the attendants. They say their last patient was discharged yesterday. There isn't an inmate in the place. They say that Nita recovered from her automobile accident and went home this morning."

"My God," Wentworth groaned, "there must be something there to show the deviltry they've been up to. Stella Flood didn't lie."

Kirkpatrick laughed harshly. "Stella Flood? The attendants say that she was a mental case, along with Anne Hale. They say that both of the girls escaped, and that Tootsler and the other keepers followed Stella to Laskar's place to try to bring her back. They claim that Tootsler's confession wasn't a confession at all, but that he was just admitting everything she said in order to humor her into coming back. From what they say, it appears that you—I mean the Spider—had no right to shoot them. They were just doing their duty—"

Wentworth groaned. "God, Kirk, you don't believe all that—"

"Frankly, Dick, I don't. But there isn't an iota of proof here to the contrary. And I'm in a hell of a spot. I ordered this raid without waiting for a search warrant, and now Kesten has a good cause against me for unlawful search—"

"Wait, Kirk! I've got proof that Kesten's place is everything Stella Flood claims it to be—"

He paused as Anne Hale got up from her chair, put a hand over the mouthpiece. "No, no, Mr. Wentworth. You mustn't tell him I'm here. I have good reasons—"

He frowned. "What reasons? Don't you realize that the lives of many people are at stake?"

"I'll explain. Hang up—"

"Not on your life! I'm going to tell Kirkpatrick to come here!" He wrested the instrument out of her hand, started to speak into it.

Anne Hale exclaimed desperately: "If you tell him I'm here, I swear I won't talk! I'll say it's all a lie, that I was never kidnapped at all!"

Wentworth looked up, almost unbelievingly, into her face. "You'd leave Nita and the others to die, or be disfigured?"

"But don't you see, the police haven't found anything! What good would it do me to talk now? It wouldn't help them to find Nita and the others. You must trust me, Mr. Wentworth, as I've trusted you. Please!"

Kirkpatrick was barking into the phone: "Well, Dick? Talk up, man? What have you got? Hello, hello, I've been dis—"

"No, no, Kirk!" Wentworth suddenly reached a decision. "All right, Anne, I'll trust you!" he whispered.

Into the instrument he spoke: "Sorry, Kirk, I'll need more

time. I'll get that proof for you, before morning. You'll have to stage another raid."

Kirkpatrick growled: "Look here, Dick, if you're hiding anything—"

"You've got to play with me this time, Kirk," Wentworth pleaded. "You were wrong about Nita, weren't you? Give me a break. I want to save Nita more than you do—"

"All right, Dick. I'll give you the break. In the meantime, I'll have to pull my men out of here."

Wentworth hung up, then faced Anne Hale. "Talk!" he rapped. "I'm trusting you with the life of Nita van Sloan!"

ANNE HALE burst out: "Don't you see, Mr. Wentworth, that Kesten must have some other place where he keeps his prisoners? I was blindfolded all the time, so I didn't know where I was. I escaped because there was some sort of commotion upstairs, and the man who was guarding me went up to see what was the matter. I pulled off the blindfold, and found myself in a dark passageway. I followed it blindly, in the darkness, and came to a stairway. I climbed the stairs, and found myself under a cellar door. I pushed up the door, climbed out, and I was on Fifth Avenue. That place must be honeycombed with secret passageways. Kesten must have moved his prisoners. They were taking me down to put into some sort of grinding machine, that would crush me to a pulp, and then they were going to put the remains in a vat of lye."

Wentworth was still cold. "But what has all this to do with your making a statement to the police?"

"That's why I didn't go directly to them. I—I had heard some of the men talking about a Ben Laskar, who was the contact man for the Spider. I—was looking for Laskar's office when you found me on Broadway. When I saw the police in front of the building, I knew that I was too late, and I told the cabby to drive on."

"I still don't see—"

"Let me go on in my own way. Today is the twenty-fifth of January. My contract with Douglas Fenner, my producer, calls for a forfeiture of one hundred thousand dollars if I should absent myself from the theatre for a period of two months continuously. I've posted a bond for that amount, and today is the last day. If I don't appear—"

Wentworth was listening to her only with half his mind. He was picturing Nita on an operating table, with the diabolical Kesten slicing at her with a keen-edged scalpel. But abruptly, Anne Hale's words penetrated his consciousness.

"It's not the hundred thousand dollars that I care about, Mr. Wentworth. *But don't you see? Douglas Fenner has everything to gain by having me kept away from the theatre tonight?*"

Richard Wentworth snapped to attention. *"Douglas Fenner!* You think he's—"

"I don't know—yet. But I want to appear at the theatre tonight. I want to go on with the show. My contract says that, if I do not give *one complete performance* in any two-month period, the bond is forfeited, *no matter what the reason!*"

Her voice dropped. "That is why I was looking for the Spider. I want to give that performance tonight, and I want the Spider to protect me!"

For a long moment Wentworth was silent. Then: "I've seen the play 'Spanish Afternoon.' Your leading man takes the part of a Spanish caballero, doesn't he?"

She nodded, breathlessly.

"All right, Miss Hale. You'll give that performance tonight. And the Spider will be there to protect you—right on the stage. In fact, the Spider is going to be your leading man tonight!"

AT EIGHT-FORTY, the Oriental Theatre was ablaze with lights as ushers escorted patrons to their seats. 'Spanish Afternoon' was about to begin. The orchestra was just reaching the last few chords of the overture, and the curtain would soon rise.

Douglas Fenner had three productions on Broadway, but this was the only one that was paying. The others all played to nearly empty houses, and kept going only by virtue of the half-price ticket agencies, which managed to dispose of enough tickets to defray part of the expenses. Fenner had been draining his profits on 'Spanish Afternoon' to carry the others, in the hope that they would catch on.

Somehow or other, word had gotten around Broadway that Anne Hale was to appear in person once more, instead of the understudy who had been taking the part. And all the elite of the Great White Way were present.

Behind the scenes, Anne Hale stood in the wings, ready to go on. She was attired as a Spanish señorita, and she appeared more beautiful than ever in the colorful costume and the tall headdress.

Beside her stood Richard Wentworth. He was costumed for the part of the leading man—in a wide-brimmed Spanish hat, and a flowing cape, with a small mask over the upper part of his face. In the play he was Don Guzman, a gay caballero under proscription by the king, daring to visit his sweetheart at the risk of his life.

An hour of intensive study had acquainted him with the cues of the first act, and he carried sheets containing his speeches sewed to the lining of his cape, where he could glance at them from time to time.

Douglas Fenner stood behind him, and the producer's face was as white and pasty as it had been the other night, when the Spider had found him at his doorstep, viewing the grisly return of Dr. Peter Humphries.

Fenner was shivering as with the ague. He leaned close to Wentworth and whispered: "I think this is very foolish of you, Spider. I don't think you should allow Miss Hale to appear. If she has enemies, they will have a grand chance at her—"

He was interrupted by the rising of the curtain.

Anne Hale moved out on to the stage, engaged in a conversation with a minor actor who had appeared from the wings at the other side. She sang a sorrowful, pretty love song, and then Fenner nudged Wentworth.

"That's your cue, Spider. For God's sake, be careful!"

Fenner did not know that the Spider was Richard Wentworth. Wentworth had come to the theatre early, had talked with the leading man, and had arranged with him for the substitution. Then he had entered Fenner's office, caped and masked as the caballero, and had introduced himself as the Spider.

"You are under suspicion, Fenner," he had said sternly. "You will either agree to this, or I will know that you are in league with Kesten. Quickly now—what is your decision?"

Fenner protested that it would ruin the play, would ruin him. But Wentworth had been obdurate, and Fenner had finally consented. It was as Wentworth had wanted it. He wanted Fenner to know that Anne Hale was appearing in person, and he wanted the man to know that he was the Spider. He was deliberately baiting a trap—and Anne Hale and he were the bait.

Now, at Fenner's nudge, Wentworth stepped out on the stage, bowed as the applause rippled up from the orchestra, and started to cross toward the center of the stage, where Anne Hale stood.

His eyes were not on Anne Hale, but on the orchestra seat, on the boxes, on the balcony. That an attack would come he was positive. But from where?

It was Anne Hale who first saw it, whose startled glance warned him.

Wentworth swung swiftly, and caught sight of activity in both the balcony boxes. In each of those boxes, a man was standing, gripping a wicked submachine gun. Behind each of those gunners, another thug, with drawn revolver, threatened the people in the other boxes, forcing them to remain motionless.

The attack had come!

And its daring simplicity should have assured its success. Those machine gunners could mow down Anne Hale and the Spider, and escape before the panic-stricken audience would be able to stop them.

WENTWORTH SWUNG into blinding action almost simultaneously with the machine-gunners in the boxes. His two hands crossed under his cloak, and emerged each gripping an automatic.

The two machine-guns were already chattering, and the first blasts of lead were ripping into the floor-boards of the stage as Wentworth fired, without even uncrossing his hands. The dull thunder of his two guns mingled with the sharp staccato barks of the machine-guns, and with the terrified screams of the audience.

Wentworth fired only four times. The first two shots disposed of the machine-gunners, the next two of the two thugs who assisted them.

Thunder echoed through every part of the theatre as the echoes of the shots died away. The people in the audience looked on aghast, not understanding how that lone man on the stage could have survived the duel against the machine-guns. But there he stood, straight, erect, a thin smile visible under the mask, as twin streams of gray smoke spiraled from his still hot guns.

A machine-gun clattered down into the orchestra pit, released by the lifeless hand of one of the dead men in the box above. A woman shrieked, and a man began to laugh loudly, raucously, hysterically. The whole thing had begun so unexpectedly, had ended so swiftly, that the audience could almost believe it had not happened.

Anne Hale had run upstage, and was crouching low, watching the Spider. Wentworth whirled, waved to her, and ran into the wings. He pushed through the crowd of actors gathered there, and headed directly for Fenner's office. Outside, he stood silent for a moment, while the uproar from the front of the theatre reached him with increasing intensity. In a moment police would be here, to question, perhaps to hold him. But he remained, listening to the high-pitched, panicky voice of Fenner, audible to him through the flimsy door. Fenner must be speaking on the phone.

"It failed, Doc!" he was shouting. "The plan failed! The Spider shot it out with them, killed them! Now, what'll I do—"

Wentworth waited for no more. He burst into the room, and Fenner screamed, threw down the phone, reached into his drawer, brought out a gun. "I'm ruined!" he screamed. "Kesten promised me she wouldn't come back till the bond was forfeited. I paid him fifty thousand dollars. Now she's back, I'm ruined—"

Viciously he brought up the gun. "And you did it, damn you, Spider—"

Before he could pull the trigger, Wentworth fired once. The gun dropped from Fenner's nerveless fingers as he fell back into the chair, a bullet through his brain.

Wentworth whirled, raced to the stage entrance, and pushed aside the doorman who tried to block his egress. In the street, a police car was just turning the corner from Broadway. Wentworth discarded his cape, mask and hat, and strode out, mingling with the excited crowd in the street. As the police car pulled up to the stage entrance, he faded into the night.

He walked two blocks, entered a drug store, and phoned headquarters. "Kirkpatrick!" he demanded. "Quick!"

"Kirk? I've failed again. Look here, you've got to try another raid on Kesten's place... What—you won't without evidence?

By God, Kirk, I've got the evidence. Get over to the Oriental Theatre. Trace the call that Fenner was making when I killed him... Yes, *I* killed him... You can send me to the chair for it if you want to, but *stage that raid first!* Get yourself a search warrant this time. No, I won't see you now, but if you'll let me run the raid for you, I'll give myself up afterwards—you have my word for it!"

"And how about the Spider?" Kirkpatrick demanded. "Will he give himself up too?"

Wentworth's voice was bitter. Nita's life was at stake. "If the raid fails, Kirk," he said slowly, "I'll promise you that the Spider will give himself up, too!"

Kirkpatrick's voice was a bit shaky. "You love her a whole lot, don't you, Dick? All right, it's a bargain. I'll have my men there. Name the hour. And the party's yours!"

CHAPTER 10
THE MASK FALLS

A LONE milk wagon rumbled through the streets, swinging into Fifth Avenue, then turning into a side street a block above the street where was located the building of the Kesten Sanatorium.

The driver of that milk wagon was well-set up, muscular, so that he bulged through the white coat. His face was not that of the contented workman starting on his early morning deliveries. Rather, it was set and hard, the face of a fighter who finds himself facing great odds.

Richard Wentworth was going to gamble that night—gamble

for high stakes. Those stakes were his life, the life of Nita van Sloan, and the lives of a dozen other prisoners of Doctor Kesten.

He pulled his wagon in to the curb, in front of a police car. Commissioner Kirkpatrick alighted from the official automobile, and met him on the sidewalk. No longer was Kirkpatrick antagonistic or blustering.

"Dick," he said, "I want to apologize for yesterday morning. I went off half-cocked, trying to force my way into your house to arrest Nita. The dictograph record of Tootsler's confession clears her completely—"

"All right, Kirk," Wentworth smiled fleetingly. "We'll let bygones be bygones. Now tell me quickly—what about the raid?"

As they talked, other shadowy figures began to materialize up and down the street.

"I've got a hundred men here this morning." He looked at his watch. "Three o'clock. That's when I told them to report. We're all set, if you are, Dick."

"That's enough!" Wentworth exclaimed. "I'm starting. Keep your men well out of sight, Kirk, and don't send them in unless you get a signal. If you hear gunfire, that'll be plenty of signal!"

He shook hands with Kirkpatrick, mounted into the milk wagon, and clucked to the horse. He drove around the corner, into the block where the sanatorium was located. Now he was sharply watchful, his eyes scanning the entire block. The sanatorium itself was dark, apparently deserted. There were no other lights anywhere on the block at this hour, except in a house some fifty yards up the street from the sanatorium. Outside shutters were closed upon most of the windows in that house, but here and there a sliver of light filtered through.

Wentworth's eyes narrowed. This might be something that the police had overlooked. However, he let that go for future consideration. Now all his attention was concentrated upon the sanatorium itself. He halted the horse in front of the building, began to whistle in a minor key as he descended with a rack of milk bottles in his hand.

He was the typical milkman now, covering his morning route. But once he had passed within the shadows of the doorway of the sanatorium, his manner changed. He had a set of passkeys all ready in his hand, and he tried one after the other. The third worked, and he pushed the door open, passed into the foyer, closing the door carefully behind him.

Almost at once a switch clicked, and the brilliant, blinding lights of the institution sprang into life. Wentworth stopped stock still, facing the uniformed attendant who stood near the light switch, covering him with a gun.

The attendant grinned nastily. "Well, wise guy, what's the answer? What's the idea of breakin' in?"

"Breaking in?" Wentworth seemed surprised. "I'm just delivering the milk!" He lifted one of the bottles from the rack in his right hand, as if to prove the truth of his statement.

The attendant grinned. "Nix, pal. You ain't no milkman. Come on an' see the boss!"

The attendant motioned toward the rear of the hall, where Wentworth could see an open sliding panel in the wall.

"You first, pal!" the attendant ordered.

"Sure," Wentworth said, and swung the milk bottle up and down in a vicious short arc. The bottom edge of the bottle caught the attendant on the forehead, cracked his skull like an eggshell. The man went down, remained motionless.

Wentworth grimly dropped his milk bottles, drew one of his automatics and approached the sliding door in the rear wall. He saw the same stairway that Kesten had descended the day before, and went down, found the passageway. He followed this, using his fountain pen flashlight, until he reached the end. And here fortune favored him again. The sliding door at the other end was also open, doubtless left that way by the attendant, so that he could return more promptly.

Wentworth made his way up the stairs, found himself in the deserted office where Kesten had told Mrs. Fleshmore her doom the day before. He moved out into the corridor, saw the open door of the operating room. This time it was occupied. A girl lay upon the table, and a man in surgical gown and mask was operating upon her!

As Wentworth approached, the man turned away from the table, saw him. It was Doctor Kesten!

Kesten snatched up a gun from the instrument table, but Wentworth, with no mercy in his heart, fired first. His slug got Kesten in the heart, and the doctor toppled backward.

Wentworth raced into the room, and looked down at the pale figure of Nita van Sloan upon the operating table. She had not been given an anesthetic, and her eyes were wide open with horror. She was strapped to the table, and there was a red, short gash under her right breast, where Kesten had begun his diabolical operation.

"Dick!" she exclaimed. "Thank God you've come!

"Just in time," Wentworth replied grimly. "Are you all right?"

"Yes, yes. The others, Dick—you'll save them?"

Wentworth nodded. "Kirk's outside, with a big raiding force. But we've got to move fast—before these other devils wake up!"

Swiftly Wentworth unstrapped her, helped her off the table. She snatched up a sheet to cover herself with, while Wentworth bent and ripped the surgical mask from Kesten's face. They both gasped.

The face of the dead man was that of Peter Humphries, the physician!

"Of course!" Wentworth exclaimed. "Humphries substituted a leper for himself, so that he would not be suspected. He was thought to be a victim, along with Johnson and the others!"

Now there was work to do. Wentworth, under Nita's direction, raced through the room with the cages, releasing the prisoners from their glass cells. They all trooped out into the street, and just then the remaining attendants, who had been in the upper floors of the building all this time, noticed the exodus. Machine guns and rifles barked down at the pitiful fugitives in the street, and Wentworth traded lead with the thugs upstairs, while the prisoners he had rescued raced to safety.

Now, from down the street, the police under Kirkpatrick made their appearance, and Kirkpatrick waved to Wentworth frantically to get out of the way. The other prisoners were safely sheltered in doorways now, but he and Nita would be caught between two cross-fires.

Wentworth seized Nita's arm, dragged her up onto the milk wagon under a hail of lead from the thugs in the upper floors, and raced the horse to the corner, while the police took over the business of mopping up the building.

It was all over in fifteen minutes, and Kirkpatrick came over to where Wentworth stood with his arms around Nita.

The Commissioner put out his hand.

"Will you shake with me, Dick?" he asked. "I was wrong from the start."

Wentworth gave him his quick smile. "Glad you admit it, Kirk. The trouble is, you never remember!"

Kirkpatrick smiled ruefully. "I'll remember from now on, Dick," he said fervently.

www.ingramcontent.com/pod-product-compliance
Lightning Source LLC
Chambersburg PA
CBHW020137180626
46810CB00004B/1600